Antiques Ravin'

Antiques Ravin'

A Trash 'n' Treasures Mystery

Barbara Allan

KENSINGTON BOOKS
www.kensingtonbooks.com

KENSINGTON BOOKS are published by

Kensington Publishing Corp.
119 West 40th Street
New York, NY 10018

All Kensington titles, imprints, and distributed lines are available at special quantity discounts for bulk purchases for sales promotion, premiums, fund-raising, educational, or institutional use. Special book excerpts or customized printings can also be created to fit specific needs. For details, write or phone the office of the Kensington Special Sales Manager: Attn. Special Sales Department. Kensington Publishing Corp., 119 West 40th Street, New York, NY 10018. Phone: 1-800-221-2647.

Kensington and the K logo Reg. U.S. Pat. & TM Off.

Library of Congress Card Catalogue Number: 2018912549

ISBN-13: 978-1-4967-1140-3
ISBN-10: 1-4967-1140-8
First Kensington Hardcover Edition: May 2019

ISBN-13: 978-1-4967-1142-7 (ebook)
ISBN-10: 1-4967-1142-4 (ebook)

10 9 8 7 6 5 4 3 2 1

Printed in the United States of America

In Memory of

Karen Lou Jensen
Beloved Aunt
1937–2018

Brandy's quote:

Three things cannot long stay hidden:
the sun, the moon, and the truth.

—Buddha

Mother's quote:

The boundaries which divide Life from Death
are at best shadowy and vague.
Who shall say where the one ends,
and where the other begins?

—Edgar Allan Poe

Chapter One

Poe, Tallyho!

The dog days of August had arrived in Serenity, our sleepy little Iowa town nestled on the banks of the Mississippi River. Even at this early Thursday morning hour, inside our two-story stucco house with the air conditioner going full blast, I could tell it was going to be another hot and humid day.

At the moment, Mother and I were having breakfast in the dining room at the Duncan Phyfe table, with Sushi on the floor next to me, waiting for any bites that I might drop by accident or on purpose. Sushi's idea of "dog days" is a 365-days-a-year proposition, in which heat and humidity are not a factor.

Mother is Vivian Borne, midseventies, Danish stock, her attractiveness hampered only slightly by large, out-of-fashion glasses that magnify her eyes; widowed, bipolar, and a legendary local thespian, she is even more legendary in our environs as an amateur sleuth.

I am Brandy Borne, thirty-three, blonde by choice, a Prozac-popping prodigal daughter who postdivorce (my bad) crawled home from Chicago to live with Mother, seeking solitude and relaxation but finding herself (which is to say myself) the frequent if reluctant accomplice in Vivian Borne's mystery-solving escapades.

Sushi, whom you've already encountered, is my adorable diabetic shih tzu, whose diabetes-ravaged eyesight was restored by a cataract operation. Perhaps the smartest of our little trio, she is still taking daily insulin injections in trade for sugar-free treats.

For newbies just joining in—heaven help you. Life in Serenity isn't always serene, nor is it uneventful, making catching you up in detail impractical. (Fortunately, all previous entries in these ongoing murder-mystery memoirs are in print.) Suffice to say, best fasten your seat belt low and tight and just come along for the ride. That's what I do.

Longtime readers will recall that at the close of *Antiques Wanted*, Mother had been the only candidate left standing in the election for county sheriff, a race she won in a walk because it was too late for any last-minute competition. She won despite a write-in campaign launched by Serenity's Millennials for John Oliver, the comedian/commentator of *Last Week Tonight*.

This irritated Mother no end. "He's *British*," she said again and again.

By the way, not revealing who I voted for is my constitutional right. I believe it's called pleading the Fifth.

Mother's breakfast today was a typically Spartan one—grapefruit juice and coffee. Mine wasn't—pancakes with whipped cream and strawberries, bacon, orange juice, and coffee—but if ever a morning called for sugar rush, protein, vitamin C, and caffeine, this was it.

Between bites, I asked, "How's the new communications system working?"

To my astonishment—and probably that of most townsfolk—Mother had kept her campaign promise to combine the separate dispatching systems of the police, sheriff, and fire departments into a single state-of-the art center to handle all three, making the routing of 911 calls to the appropriate responder quicker and more efficient.

And she had done this—as also promised—at no cost to the taxpayers. How? By relentlessly going after grants for law enforcement, and persuading—let's not call it blackmail, shall we?—state representatives to assist her. These politicians knew that *she* knew they had skeletons in their closets they might not want to come rattling out. Okay, maybe call it blackmail . . . but implied blackmail.

Blackmail with a smile.

Mother, after taking a sip of coffee, replied, "The new com sys is strictly 10-2. Thank you for asking, dear!"

"Ten to what? What are you talking about?"

"10-2 is the police code for 'signal good.' You should familiarize yourself with all of them. I'll provide a cheat sheet!"

She removed a napkin from her collar, as if she was the one chowing down like a lumberjack. Serenity's new sheriff was dressed in a uniform of her own design, having tried on and rejected the scratchy, polyester ill-fitting one used by her predecessor, Pete Rudder. (To be clear, not the actual uniform he'd worn, but one supposedly in her size and for a female officer, though you'd never guess it.)

Anyway, Mother had contacted her favorite clothing company, Breckenridge, and—don't ask me how—talked someone there into making several stylish jumpsuits of tan cotton/elastane with just the faintest hint of lavender, featuring plentiful pockets, epaulettes, and subtle shoulder pads. The outfits also had horizontal nylon zippers at the elbows and knees that turned them into a cooler (tempwise) version when unzipped, which was how she was comfortably wearing one this steaming morning. (She still had the legs for it, and once a year she had any spider veins zapped.)

I said, "I'm surprised you followed through with it."

Mother, about to take a sip of juice, frowned. "Followed through with what, dear?"

"The new communications center—especially one set up so that the public doesn't have access to it."

In the past, Mother had been able to walk into the PD and up to the Plexiglas, establish a rapport with the latest dispatcher, discover his or her weakness, then exploit those frailties to wheedle out confidential police information.

She gave me a smug little smile. "Well, dear, I'm on the *inside* now, and privy to everything."

I grunted. When her term of office ended, Mother might well come to regret the upgrade. If she ran a second time, she would hardly be the only candidate for sheriff.

Her radio communicator, resting on the table, squawked, and she answered it.

"10-4, Deputy Chen," she said.

Deputy Charles Chen was her right-hand man. I feel sure that Charles's restaurateur parents were unaware of how close Chen was to Chan. Or maybe not—certainly nobody called the handsome young deputy Charlie.

"Businesses in Antiqua got broken into overnight."

"A 10-14!"

"You want me to respond, Sheriff?"

"No, dear," Mother told him. "And do please call me Vivian. And now I'm off to Antiqua! It's time their mayor met the new county sheriff."

"Okay."

"I believe you mean 10-4, dear."

The radio communicator clicked at her. She gave it a mildly offended look, then put it down, and—eyes gleaming behind the large lenses—announced, "Time for us to roll, Brandy!"

What did I have to do with rolling, you may ask?

Well, due to her various vehicular infractions—including but not limited to driving across a cornfield and knocking over a mailbox, both while off her medication—Sheriff Vivian Borne had no driver's license . . . well, actually she did, it just had REVOKED stamped on it.

Since the department couldn't spare a deputy just to haul her around, and the budget couldn't afford the cost of an outside driver, she'd arm-twisted me into playing unpaid chauffeur.

And I wasn't happy about it.

We'd had to temporarily close our antiques shop, Trash 'n' Treasures—an old house where each room was devoted to antiques that thematically belonged there—but I guess that was okay, since August was always a slow month for sales, often more money going out than coming in. Still, schlepping Mother around town and countryside was not my idea of a summer vacation.

Sushi had also been pressed into service, riding along with us, partly because the little furball was so cute and disarming. She was bound to put most people at ease when the sheriff came a-callin'.

But Soosh could also be very vindictive when left home alone for long periods of time—more than once Mother and I had returned to find a small cigar left in the foyer.

Mother had a little jumpsuit made for her doggie deputy, as well, which got only one day's wear before it was found shredded in the upstairs hallway, a mystery with no doubt as to who-done-it. I'd escaped any such indignity, my chauffeur's uniform being my own sundresses and sandals.

I had made it clear to Mother that my role was to be strictly ex officio. I wanted no uniform or badge or official designation. Anyway, what could sound more ridiculous than "Deputy Brandy"?

While I cleared the table, Mother put on one of her two duty belts. She had a heavy one for serious situations, containing separate holders for her gun, nightstick, taser, handcuffs, mace, flashlight, and radio, plus pouches for bullets, Swiss Army knife, and latex gloves, and a lighter belt for investigations (like now), which included only holders for the radio, flashlight, and handcuffs, plus a large pouch for carrying antipsychotic pills, aspirin, antacids, allergy tablets, arthritis cream, eye drops, laxatives, lip balm, and dog treats to make canine friends. (She wanted to take all of her vitamins along as well, but the pouch wouldn't close, and I purposely used a little cross-body purse so she couldn't load me down.) She had as yet never worn her heavier rig with sidearm, as it ruined the line of her uniform.

I was exhausted already, and we hadn't even left the house.

At a quarter to eight, Mother, Sushi, and I made the trek all the way outside and were immediately engulfed in oppressive heat. We trudged dutifully to her sheriff's car parked in the driveway, doing our best not to wilt.

Mother had been given the choice of either a four-door Ford Taurus or a hatchback Ford Explorer. Both were white with sky-blue sheriff's markings and the same policing equipment: in-car video system with monitor (mounted to the right of the rearview mirror), mobile data terminal (between the front seats and angled toward Mother), mobile radio system (beneath the dashboard), and standard steel mesh/Plexiglas barrier (between the front and back seats). There was also a bunch of hardware in the way-back, like a battering ram (not as easy to use as seen on TV), and a canvas bag carrying a gas mask, protective boots, extra flashlights, and other items.

Since I wasn't an official law enforcement officer, I was

prohibited from using any of this equipment, even if I knew how, which I didn't. Nor did I have any desire to.

Being the designated driver, I had lobbied for the Taurus, feeling more comfortable behind its wheel. But Mother chose the Explorer, which I'd presumed was because the larger vehicle looked more formidable and had four-wheel drive. The real reason for her preference for the SUV had soon become apparent; yesterday, she spotted a rusty metal 1950s lawn chair by the roadside and commanded me to pull over and take custody of it, meaning put it in the hatchback.

Yes, folks, that's what I'm dealing with. And who the good people of Serenity County have protecting them.

Anyway, with me behind the wheel, Sushi on Mother's lap as the sheriff rode shotgun (not literally, though there was one in back), we headed out of Serenity—no siren wailing or lights flashing (that's 10-85, according to my cheat sheet)—bound for Antiqua.

Our destination was not a Caribbean island but a little town located in the far western section of the county, just off Interstate 80, its sole industry the many antiques shops drawing tourists from all over the Midwest. Antiqua wasn't large enough to have its own police force, contracting instead with the county sheriff's department to provide certain services—like patrolling the area, investigating crimes, handling traffic, and offering crime prevention classes . . . every service provided at a cost, of course.

To stay awake after the heavy breakfast, I asked, "How come we've never gone to Antiqua looking for merchandise? Sounds like it would be right up the Trash 'n' Treasures alley."

We'd made any number of trips to little towns around the region on buying expeditions, starting back in the days when we had a stall in an antiques mall, prior to our shopkeeper phase.

"Because even with our dealer's discount," Mother said, "the prices are too high."

When it came to hunting for bargains, Mother wasn't just a bottom feeder, she was a subterranean gorger.

She went on: "Some of the shops in Antiqua used to be reasonable, and the occasional bargain could be sniffed out . . . but that was before Poe's Folly."

What do you think? Should I ask? Are you sure? Well . . . all right. But the responsibility is yours.

"What on earth," I asked, "is Poe's Folly?"

"Why, I'm surprised you've never heard of that, dear. It made news some years back. Quite a kerfuffle!"

I guess I'd been preoccupied with my own folly back in Chicago.

"One of the antique shops," she continued, "sold a small framed photo to a tourist for ninety dollars."

"That sounds a little high, but not the makings of anything newsworthy."

Mother lifted a finger. "Actually, it was a newsworthy *bargain*—a daguerreotype dating to 1850 that turned out to be a rare portrait of Edgar Allan Poe himself. The store was crammed with so much stuff, the owners apparently didn't know what they had."

"So it was worth *more* than ninety dollars?"

"How about fifty-thousand simoleons."

"Ouch!"

Mother continued, "Needless to say, the incident—indeed dubbed 'Poe's Folly' by the media—was quite an embarrassment to the town, especially since the buyer took the picture to a taping of *Antiques Roadshow* in Des Moines, where the Antiqua shop's costly blunder was exposed to eight and a half million viewers."

I smirked. "Must've been pretty embarrassing to the person who sold it. Of course, it might encourage bargain hunters to drop by his shop."

"One might think. But in fact it only called into question the shop owner's ability to price anything correctly. He took it quite hard."

"I thought any publicity was good publicity."

"Apparently not, dear. The man killed himself." She went on cheerfully, death never anything that brought her down. "Anyhoo, after the Folly became so widely known, prices skyrocketed all over town. No one wanted to make the same mistake twice!"

"Understandable," I said, "but probably not good for business."

She fluttered a hand. "Oh, initially it had no effect, because bargain hunters came from hither and yon. But when nothing of significance was discovered beyond outrageous price tags, tourism dropped off significantly." She paused. "Then a few years back, the town council concocted a plan to turn their folly into fortune."

"How'd they do that?" We were zipping along the Interstate now, despite truck-heavy traffic.

"The first weekend in August, Antiqua holds 'Edgar Allan Poe Days,' a gala three-day celebration with festivities beginning on Friday."

"Well, that's tomorrow," I pointed out.

"Yes, and the pièce de résistance is a hunt for an authentic Poe collectible marked at a ridiculously low price."

"Like that daguerreotype photo?"

"Nothing quite so valuable, dear, but still worth a pretty penny. An ingenious gimmick to embrace its famous folly, don't you think?"

"Yes, but it must be tough coming up with Poe items like that."

"Not really. Everyone on the town council is an antiques dealer with beaucoup connections. Last year's treasure was a short missive Eddie Poe had written to a friend about a change of address, worth several thousand . . . priced at a mere twenty-five dollars."

"Not too shabby," I said. "How come we've never attended?"

Mother sniffed. "Because, dear, the first year the festival was held I wrote to the city council and offered to perform 'The Raven' at the opening ceremony, in full costume and makeup!"

"As what, a raven?"

"Don't be ridiculous, dear! As *Poe*, of course. I look rather dashing in a mustache. And can you imagine? I never heard boo back from them!" She was getting miffed about it all over again, enough so to get a curious upward look from Soosh. "Well, I *swore* to myself I would darken Antiqua's door, nevermore!"

"But now you're sheriff and you have to."

"And now they will see just who it was they snubbed!"

She didn't just hold a grudge, she caressed it, nurtured it . . .

Fairly familiar with Poe's work, I said, "Maybe the issue was what a long poem 'The Raven' is. Maybe if you had offered up a shorter one, like 'Annabel Lee' or 'The City in the Sea' . . ."

But she was snoring.

Serenity County's new sheriff was starting her day off with a nap, as was the out-of-uniform deputy Sushi, curled in her lap.

The lady sleeps! Oh, may her sleep, which is enduring, so be deep!

I returned my attention to the road, where the gently rolling hills had been replaced with flat farmland, fields of tall green corn swaying seductively in the breeze, tassels ready for pollination.

Half an hour later, an exit sign to Antiqua appeared and

I turned off the Interstate onto a secondary road, where a two-pump gas station kept company with a cut-rate motel.

Soon a larger sign greeted me:

WELCOME TO ANTIQUA!

ANTIQUES CAPITAL
OF THE MIDWEST
POPULATION 354

The asphalt highway became cobblestone Antiques Drive, where well-kept houses on either side—newer ones on the outskirts, older but grander homes more centrally located—wore well-tended lawns in civic pride.

I passed a tree-shaded park with a large pond, several log-cabin-style picnic shelters, and a perfunctory playground, all deserted at this early hour. As I breezed on in to the small downtown, Mother and Sushi snored on.

I slowed the Explorer along the main drag to rubberneck at the quaint Victorian brick buildings decorated with colorful floral planters—some hanging, others in urns—each business displaying its merchandise behind gleaming windows. Most were antiques stores, but among them was a café, and bakery, and gift shop.

After three blocks, the downtown turned residential again—houses not quite so nice now, but lawns still welcoming—and I backtracked along side streets, where significantly more modern buildings maintained the town's service industries: drugstore, bar, restaurant, and a branch bank.

A one-story clapboard church with small bell tower, which could have been built ten years ago or one hundred, was relegated to a side street as well; next to it lay an old cemetery that probably dated back to the founding of the town.

I was about to swing onto Antiques Drive again when a man in a pale yellow polo shirt and tan slacks ran into the street and flagged me down. He was smiling but something frantic was in it.

I stopped and powered down the window, which was akin to opening a hot oven door.

"Ah . . . Sheriff?" the man asked, frowning. He was mid-sixties, silver-haired and distinguished looking (in a country-club way), and wore wire-framed glasses. Perhaps a sweet young thing like myself, in a sundress, was not what he was expecting.

"That would be her," I said, nodding to the uniformed if slumbering Mother, a little drool oozing from her open mouth.

I poked her arm, and she woke up with a snort, echoed by Sushi. They looked at me with identical dazed expressions.

"What?" Mother mumbled. "Where?"

"10-23," I chirped, which meant we'd arrived at the scene, then I turned back to the man. "Where do you want her?"

I admit it sounded as if I was dropping off a potted plant.

"There," he said, pointing across the street to a one-story tan brick building, a sign above the entrance reading CITY HALL. Nothing antique or Victorian about the place, strictly modern-day institutional.

"We've been waiting for you," he went on, a tinge of irritation in his voice, which I attributed to the heat rather than any perceived tardiness on our part; we'd made good time—for not using the siren, anyway.

He turned and headed toward the building while I pulled the car over to the curb.

Shutting off the engine, I said, "Hope city hall is air-conditioned."

Mother was giving me a hard glare of a stare.

"What?" I asked.

"You *could* have woken me up!"

"I did wake you up."

"You could have woken me up *sooner*." She was drying her mouth off with a hanky. "I had hoped to make a lasting first impression."

"Well, you succeeded."

We exited the vehicle, Mother carrying Sushi like a suspect she was hauling to the clink.

The interior of city hall was as dull and institutional as the exterior, with beige walls and tan-tiled floor. A large metal desk protected the offices of city officials behind it. On the desk was a multiline phone and a silver bell with RING FOR SERVICE, which suggested that city hall had trouble keeping a receptionist.

The silver-haired man who'd flagged us down held out a hand to Mother. "I'm Myron Hatcher, the mayor, owner of Top Drawer Antiques."

Mother transferred Sushi to me and then shook the hand.

"Sheriff Vivian Borne," she said majestically, not a speck of drool in sight. "And this is my ad hoc deputy, Brandy Borne. My daughter." She summoned a forced smile. "If a president can hire his family, so can I!"

I didn't care for the deputy designation, ad hoc or otherwise, but had no need to embarrass her—she could handle that without my help.

When the mayor's hand went to me, I transferred Sushi back to Mother and shook with him.

All this transferring had annoyed Sushi, who growled and squirmed out of Mother's arms.

Mr. Hatcher was saying, "Please come on back."

We skirted around the big desk and proceeded down the beige hallway, passing doors reading MAYOR, TREASURER, and ADMINISTRATOR. At one marked CONFERENCE, our host opened the door, and we proceeded in, Sushi trotting in last.

The bulk of the room was taken up by an oval-shaped table with chairs for about a dozen, four of which were occupied by two men and two women.

"Sheriff," Mr. Hatcher said, "I'd like you to meet the members of the city council."

Mother nodded regally to them, a queen to her court. "I would like that myself."

Since I was now out of the conversation, I parked myself on a small couch in the corner, where Sushi soon joined me.

The mayor began the introductions.

The council consisted of Lottie Everhart, late forties, long dark hair, attractive, attired in a leopard-print dress, owner of Somewhere in Time; Rick Wheeler, thirties, handsome, blond, buff in a tight white T-shirt and black jeans, manager of Treasure Aisles Antiques Mall; Wally Thorp, mid-fifties, round-faced, overweight, thinning gray hair, sporting a wrinkled short-sleeved plaid shirt and well-worn cargo shorts, proprietor of Junk 'n' Stuff; and Paula Baxter, early fifties, short dyed red hair, rather plain, in part due to scant make-up, wearing a sleeveless navy cotton dress, owner of Relics Antiques.

With the preamble concluded, Mother took a chair next to Paula while the mayor put a few empty seats between himself and the others.

"Now," Mother said, "who wants to fill me in?"

The council members deferred to the mayor.

"As far as we can tell," Myron said, "our five shops were entered through their back doors sometime last night."

Mother nodded. "What about security systems?"

Rick said sourly, "They don't do any good when the sheriff's department is an hour away."

"A valid point," Mother conceded. "Though just a loud

alarm *can* be helpful. Have you been able to determine what was stolen?"

Paula turned up both palms. "*Nothing* seems to have been taken from my place."

"Or mine," added Lottie.

"Same here," Myron said.

Wally, the junk store owner, smirked. "It would take me a week of Sundays to take stock of my stock."

Mother looked at Rick. "What about you, young man?"

"I've contacted all my dealers in the mall," he said with a shrug, "but most haven't had a chance to take an inventory yet." His eyebrows went up. "I did a walk-through and everything *looked* okay. I run a tidy ship."

Myron spoke. "Strikes us as odd, Sheriff, that our registers had cash in them to use in the morning, which went untouched. No small fortune, even combined . . . but still, why would a thief not help himself?"

"Or herself," Mother said with a grave nod.

Paula piped up. "I expected to find my glass case with expensive rings and watches broken into and emptied out, but it wasn't."

"Nor," Lottie said, "was any of my rare Roseville pottery missing."

When Mother's eyes went to Wally, he merely shrugged; apparently the junkman had nothing of real value in his store.

Mother rested her elbow on the table and her chin on a hand. "What do you think the burglar was after?"

Again, the group yielded to the mayor. "The only thing we can figure is that someone went looking for this year's Poe item . . . knowing it would be a valuable prize."

"Makes sense. And what is it?"

The question drew silence and shared wary looks within the group.

Then Myron spoke. "Sorry, Sheriff Borne . . . but we're really not at liberty to say. You see, the first of three encrypted clues as to what the Poe prize is won't be released to the public until tomorrow, at the opening ceremony."

"Myron, this is the *sheriff*," Paula chided. "I think she can be trusted with the information."

Wondering if my presence might be a problem, I offered to leave the room.

But the mayor shook his head. "Not necessary, Deputy."

Deputy. I didn't love the sound of that.

Adjusting his wire frames again, the major sighed, then said, "Very well—it's a book called *Tales*, published in 1845 by Wiley and Putnam, featuring perhaps the author's most famous story, 'The Gold-Bug.'"

Lottie sat forward. "That's where we got the idea for the encrypted clues," she said. "The first one says what the value of the item is, the second one tells what it is, and the third gives the antiques shop where it's hidden among various merchandise on display."

Eyes narrowed, Mother was taking all of this in. "It does sound as though the burglar wanted to get a jump on the competition."

"Yes," Wally said. "Only he . . . or she . . . didn't know we'd changed the procedure this year."

"How so?"

"We aren't hiding the prize until the second day of the festival," he explained.

"That's by necessity," Lottie added. "Last year, the letter was found right away, and that cast a cloud over the rest of the weekend."

Paula was nodding. "People left. And our shops didn't do at all well on a weekend that's bigger than Christmas for Antiqua."

"City hall especially suffered," the mayor added.

I heard myself ask, "Why is that?"

The mayor glanced over at me. "City hall offers deciphered clues for ten dollars a pop, and a lot of people prefer paying the cash rather than figuring out the cryptograms, which we depend on to fund the festival, and next year's prize of a Poe rarity."

Rick rolled his eyes, his expression glum. "We merchants had to dig into our own pockets this year."

The room fell silent again.

"Perhaps," Mother suggested, "you should have some law enforcement presence during the festival."

The mayor looked startled. "That might alarm folks."

I had been feeling guilty about making Mother look like a buffoon by not waking her up, so I piped up.

"Sheriff Borne does a wonderful reading of 'The Raven,'" I said. "If you asked her to perform at the opening ceremony, it would make perfect sense for her to be around all weekend. She could be an honored guest."

The council agreed my idea was a good one, and Mother sent me a grateful look.

Since the members needed to open their shops soon, the meeting came to an end, Mother shaking hands and exchanging smiles all around.

When Mother informed them she wanted to examine the rears of their shops to see how the burglar had gained entrance, I told her Sushi and I would be at a little coffee shop I'd noticed down the street.

As I trailed Mother and the group out of city hall, Lottie dropped back and handed me a slip of paper.

"Here's the encrypted first clue," she said, then added with a good-natured smile, "If you want a deciphered version, it'll cost you ten bucks."

I looked at the row of numbers and symbols . . . and coughed up the ten-spot for a second slip of paper with the solution. Even an ad hoc deputy can put in for a few expenses.

Lottie said, "The numbers and symbols are random designations of letters, but the code is consistent throughout the next two clues. So with this, you should be able to figure out the others."

A savings for the county of twenty bucks. Now I was a fiscally responsible ad hoc deputy.

The outside of the Coffee Club looked more upscale than the inside, with its worn carpet, scarred prefab tables, and cracked faux-leather padded chairs. But none of that mattered because the air-conditioning was nicely arctic.

I spotted a waitress behind the counter, early twenties, with short, spiky purple hair; alabaster skin; and purple lipstick. Just another typical small-town girl.

Still in the doorway, I asked, "Is it okay if my dog comes in?"

She shrugged. "Since the boss isn't here, sure."

I took a table for two, placing the panting Sushi in my lap.

The waitress came over. Her name tag said MORELLA, and she reeked of Shalimar perfume. Hanging from her neck on a silver chain was a pendent of a black raven, wings spread.

"And how are you?" I asked pleasantly.

"Livin' the dream. What can I get you?"

"Iced coffee . . . and maybe a little water for Sushi?"

"Right." She headed back behind the counter.

A few other customers occupied tables—two giggling teenage girls hunched over a cell phone, and a young mother with small boy, sharing a cupcake.

Morella returned, setting a sweating glass in front of me and a little bowl of water for Soosh, whose tongue flicked out and lapped up the liquid loudly.

"Thanks," I said. "Nice town."

"Don't look under the hood."

"Well, the people seem friendly enough."

One heavily filled-in eyebrow went up. "Do they?"

"So far."

"Stick around."

Bluntly, I asked, "What keeps you here?"

"As soon as I get enough money, nothing."

"Destination?"

She flicked me something that was probably a smile. "Anywhere else."

Morella put my ticket on the table, then went to check on the other customers.

While I sipped my cold drink, I spread out the two slips of paper Lottie had given me—the cryptogram and its solution.

;48 [50?8 +1 ;48 6;89 6) ;8* ;4+?)5*=

The value of the item is ten thousand

I took out a pen from my little bag to make notes, recording which random numbers and symbols stood for which letter. Even without the ten-dollar translation, the code seemed pretty easy—a semicolon equaled a "t," a 4 equaled an "h," an 8 equaled an "e" (adding up to "the"). Also, spaces between the symbols and numbers indicated separate words, which wasn't the case in "The Gold-Bug," meaning when I got the next cryptogram, I could probably (as Lottie had mentioned) save Serenity County ten bucks.

On the other hand, ten *thousand* bucks seemed like a lot for the local merchants to shell out.

I finished the iced coffee, left cash for the drink plus a generous tip to speed Morella on her way anywhere else, and Sushi and I departed.

Going back to join Mother, I crossed the side street where our Explorer was parked across from city hall.

A slip of paper pinned beneath a wiper waved hello in the warm breeze. Walking through heat shimmering off the sidewalk, I went to the vehicle and plucked off the note.

This message needed no deciphering.

> *Believe nothing you hear and only half of what you see. Edgar Allan Poe.*

A Trash 'n' Treasures Tip

When collecting rare books, first decide if you will hunt on your own or use a reputable book dealer. If you hunt on your own, you will pay less but will be *on* your own. Unless you are very well schooled in the hobby, you may mistake a later edition for a first. A dealer will hunt for you and protect you from such mistakes, but expect to pay higher prices. On the other hand, Mother once paid thirty dollars for a Rex Stout first edition worth $1,500 (books were on sale 20 percent off, and Mother insisted on her discount).

Chapter Two

Poe Show

When Mother, Sushi, and I returned to Antiqua Friday morning, we found the tiny town quite changed from the day before. The park now buzzed with activity—families occupying the picnic shelters, children cavorting on the playground, even a few rowboats gliding lazily out on the pond.

The downtown, too, brimmed with folks—parking places at a premium, sidewalks crowded—as the opening ceremony of Edgar Allan Poe Days approached. The only thing in common with yesterday was the hot and humid weather.

I parked the Explorer illegally in front of city hall, enjoying my first moment of ex officio privilege, but before we had a chance to exit the vehicle, Mayor Myron Hatcher—in a white short-sleeved shirt, blue tie, and neatly pressed navy slacks—hurried out of the building toward us.

I powered down my window.

"I believe we're going to have record attendance," he announced, his face flushed with excitement, or maybe the heat.

Mother replied regally, "Hardly a surprise. Word has clearly gotten around about my upcoming Poe-formance."

She smiled at her punny remark.

The mayor's eyes widened before he responded with political prudence, "Ah . . . yes, I'm sure that's the reason."

Mother's eyebrows rose. "Any further break-ins?"

"No," Hatcher said. "Of course, we had volunteers patrolling the streets during the night, which helped, apparently."

"Good call! Continue the practice."

The mayor went on, "I've managed to secure lodging for you—no small feat, by the way—as everything has been sold out for months."

"A suite at the local hotel?"

"If you mean the Tiki Motel . . . uh, no. I've arranged accommodations at a most *unusual* bed and breakfast." He nodded to a silver Cadillac sedan parked in a spot reserved for His Honor. "You can follow me—it's not far, but why walk in this heat?"

"Why indeed?" Mother responded, with an unnecessary flourish of a hand and bow of the head. Her theatrical mode was already encroaching upon her law enforcement role.

I trailed the Caddy a few blocks this way and that, and then Mayor Hatcher pulled into the gravel drive of a pale yellow two-story cottage with gingerbread trim and a white picket fence. It didn't look unusual to me, except perhaps unusually nice.

We got out of our vehicles, doors closing behind us as if in brief applause. Mother, gazing at our quaintly welcoming home away from home, clasped her hands. "How adorable!"

"Oh," the mayor said, batting the air dismissively, "that's not where you're staying."

He gestured, and we followed him around to the back

of the cottage where a single train car perched on what I assumed was a no-longer-in-use track line.

"What," I said, "we're hopping a freight?"

Mother turned to me. "Dear, don't be ungrateful. I think it's *simply* charming." Her head rotated to the mayor. "Anyway, that's no freight, it's a Pullman car! Isn't it, Your Honor? Which are known for being the *top* of the railroad line."

Yes, around the turn of two centuries ago.

"Come along," Hatcher said. "I think you'll be pleasantly surprised."

As we moved in tandem behind the mayor and toward the train car, he continued, "The owner of the cottage had an out-of-town conflict this year and hadn't planned on renting out the Pullman. But he entrusted me with the key to use it at my discretion."

Sushi was in my arms. "Do they allow canines on this train?" I asked.

Hatcher smiled. "I can see your dog is well behaved."

He didn't know her very well, did he? If annoyed, ignored, or just plain feeling ornery, Sushi could shred a pillow in seconds. Not to mention the damage she could do with her caboose.

I said, "I hope this thing has its brake on."

"This Pullman car doesn't have a brake," the mayor said. "But don't worry—you won't be going anywhere."

Three metal steps at the front of the train car led to a small landing encased by a black-iron railing, where the mayor unlocked an etched glass wooden door. Pushing it open, he moved aside for us to enter, and we stepped into a rectangular sitting room, awash in Victorian splendor— oriental rug, floral couch, needlepoint chairs, velvet tasseled curtains, fringed-shaded lamps. The walls gleamed of rich dark walnut, and the curved ceiling was painted a deep red.

But the best feature—as far as I was concerned—was a de-cidedly *not*-antique window air conditioner, humming along quietly, doing a fine job of keeping the quarters cool.

We continued along a narrow hallway hugging the left side of the car, passing by a little galley kitchen with modern, stainless steel conveniences; then a bathroom with a small claw-footed tub, toilet, and sink with brass fixtures; arriving at the end of the line in the bedroom, where a Victorian four-poster bed with a carved wooden canopy took up most of the space.

Since Mother's vociferous snoring might well bring the canopy down on top of us, I would of course be sleeping on the couch.

"Well?" asked Hatcher.

"Breathtaking!" Mother extolled.

And yet she still had breath to go on.

"Reminds me," she continued, "of a train trip I once took as a little girl, all by myself with a note pinned to my dress, informing interested parties that I was bound for Chattanooga. My seat was practically in the baggage car, but I snuck into first class and—"

I cut in. "Yes, Mayor Hatcher, this is *very* nice. Please extend our thanks and appreciation to the owner."

Hatcher nodded. "Will do. Here is the key." This he handed over to Mother. "Now, I imagine you'll want to unpack, and I need to get back to city hall. We're all looking forward to your performance, Mrs. Borne . . . er . . . Sheriff. Oh, one thing—you'll have to fend for yourselves for food in the morning, since your host isn't here."

So bed, but no breakfast.

"We'll muddle through," Mother said cheerfully.

"All right, then." He gave Mother a little salute. "See you at the noon ceremony, Sheriff."

He disappeared.

Mother plopped down on the bed, then bounced to test

the springs; Sushi jumped up on the coverlet to join in on the fun. They both looked comfortably situated and settled in for a brief morning nap.

Well, someone had to bring in the luggage—there didn't seem to be a porter around.

As comfy as Mother had looked on that bed, I was just that miserable, an hour or so later, seated in a folding chair in the park. Beneath the sweltering sun, surrounded by a sea of people, we were all listening to the opening ceremony speech given by the mayor, who stood on a small riser at a microphone on a stand.

For a while I feared that the four other council members might want to have their moment in the sun too, but none of them seemed to be in attendance. They were probably busy at their respective shops.

Myron Hatcher, having discarded his earlier tie, the white shirt looking more than a little damp, droned on: ". . . promising to be Antiqua's best Edgar Allan Poe Days *evermore*. . . ."

His speech was peppered with more cringe-worthy Poe puns than . . . well, than the ones you're likely to get from me in this book.

Suddenly I envied Sushi, left behind in the cool confines of the Pullman car.

Mother, standing in the shade of an oak tree, waiting her turn, must have been even more uncomfortable than yours truly. Serenity County's sheriff was cocooned in her Poe costume of black, full-length frock coat over black suit with white high-collar shirt; black silk cravat; short, curly dark wig; and mustache. She had ditched her big, thick glasses, making a public safety menace out of the sheriff.

And yet there wasn't a bead of sweat on her brow.

". . . and now, without further ado," the mayor concluded, "I'd like to introduce to you our new county sheriff, Vivian Borne, who will kick off our celebration with a rendition of 'The Raven.'"

Mother frowned, disappointed by his perfunctory introduction. Didn't he know who she was? (Obviously he did, or he wouldn't be giving her this venue.)

Polite applause followed, but also a few groans from those familiar with the length of the poem.

Hatcher took his exit, and Mother strode forward amid a mixed reaction to her getup (*ohh*s and *ahh*s, giggles and titters), the tails of the frock coat flapping. Sans her spectacles she nearly tripped up the steps to the riser, but she recovered nicely with a sweeping bow, which brought enthusiastic clapping.

Eschewing the microphone for her theatrical voice, Mother began in a male octave, which, actually, wasn't that hokey and included more than a touch of Vincent Price.

"Once upon a midnight dreary, while I pondered, weak and weary . . ."

An elderly couple in the front row struggled to their feet and began what was to be a painfully long trek up the center aisle.

". . . over many a quaint and curious volume of forgotten lore . . ."

The pair of octogenarians were close enough to Mother that I knew she could see them, though she pretended not to.

"While I nodded, nearly napping, suddenly there came a tapping . . ."

Another defector in the front row—a middle-aged woman with an expression worthy of a witness at the Hindenburg explosion—made her exit. Soon after, she was followed by her apparent husband, in a half crouch, as if he were avoiding the whirling blades of a helicopter.

While Mother had given the elderly couple (still soldiering

on) a pass, her eyes shot daggers at the backs of the middle-aged couple.

"... *as of some one gently rapping, rapping at my chamber door.*"

An excited murmur was spreading through the crowd, and when *"First clue is out!"* reached my ears, I knew many in the audience would leave, even if that raven at the window wouldn't. Or was he at the chamber door? I never quite got that.

Anyway, as the exodus began in earnest, Mother started speaking louder and faster.

" '*'Tis some visitor,*' *I muttered,* '*tapping at my chamber door—only this and nothing more.*' "

I felt pity for her, I really did, genuine sympathy; but when a heavyset lady in front of me rose, I used the woman's bulk as cover to make my own escape, like a marauder in a movie hiding behind an artificial bush.

So it was that Vivian Borne's terrible, ungrateful child hoofed it back to check on Sushi.

(We had decided to keep the Explorer parked at the Pullman, since walking anywhere in Antiqua would be faster than driving, due to the influx of cars and a scarcity even of illegal parking places. We also elected to leave the key under the doormat, since our comings and goings might occasionally be at odds.)

When I entered the Pullman, Sushi was lounging on the Victorian couch. A quick look around told me she had behaved herself—no shredded pillows, or unsmokable cigars.

"If we're smart," I said, scooping her up, "we won't be here when Mother gets back. She will *not* be in a good mood."

Sushi nodded. (I swear she did.)

So out we went.

On the way to the Coffee Club, we were passing George's

Bakery when I thought perhaps I should pick up something for breakfast.

The front of the bakery was small—one room with a long glass-encased counter, a checkout area, and a token ice-cream type table with two chairs. An open doorway led to the back kitchen.

I assumed the portly, balding man behind the cash register was the owner; about sixty, he wore a white apron speckled with various colors of frosting.

He said, apologetically, "I'm afraid there's not much left—just a couple chocolate donuts and a few muffins. I had a real rush in here this morning. A mob!"

"I'll have two muffins to go," I said, adding, "doesn't matter the kind."

"I'll just give them to you—how's that?"

"Well, thanks . . . ah . . . you're George?"

"Guilty as charged." He looked at Sushi in my arms. I wondered for half a moment if he'd scold me for bringing a canine in, but he only smiled. "How about a doggie biscuit? No charge there, either. I make 'em special with no sugar for clients with canines."

"Great."

He came out from behind the counter with a small bone-shaped cookie and put it under Sushi's nose. She snatched the treat with her jaws, chewed it up with her sharp little teeth, and barked once for another. Politely, like Oliver Twist asking, "Please, sir, I want some more."

I reprimanded her, just for show, because I already knew she had George in the palm of her paws.

George patted her furry head. "I'll put another one in the sack with the muffins."

I thanked him again, and we left.

Under normal circumstances, I would have had Sushi on her leash, walking along beside me, but with the sidewalks so crowded, I was afraid she might get stepped on.

With the festival under way, the coffee shop was busy now, the only available table a two-seater in back, which I snagged as its dishes were still being cleared by a frazzled busboy.

As I settled in with Sushi on my lap, an equally frazzled young waitress came over, long brown hair pulled back in a ponytail, her name tag reading WILLOW.

"Menu?" she asked brusquely.

"No," I said, "just an iced latte, and some water in a little dish, please."

She looked from her pad to Sushi, so—afraid she'd give us the boot—I threw in some subterfuge.

I asked, "Morella not working this morning?"

"No," Willow said sourly, "she was a no-show. And I was supposed to have the day off!"

"Maybe she finally left town."

The waitress grunted. "Sleepin' it off is more like it. Another late night at the casino, prob'ly. Anyway, she doesn't answer her cell."

"I hope she's all right," I said, pretending to be interested for Sushi's sake.

"Yeah. Excuse me, I got other orders to take."

Willow hurried off.

Seated at a table next to me were two well-dressed women, one blonde in her midthirties, the other brunette and a little older. Both had iced teas and were sharing a cheesecake.

I didn't mean to eavesdrop on their conversation, but they had to raise their voices above the café din, which made an unintended audience out of me.

"I tell you, Amy," the older one said, "we could use a whole new city council! One with not so many antique shop owners. Everything they do is designed to benefit themselves! This festival, for instance . . . mostly puts money in *their* pockets. I mean, it's not like all these visitors are here to get a haircut, or do some dry cleaning, or open a bank account."

"Jessica, that's not entirely true. The motel and bed-and-breakfasts all do well—and the restaurant and bar, too. And people might use some of the other businesses." She paused. "But, yeah, I would *rather* have had a music festival of *any* kind."

My iced latte and Sushi's water arrived, along with the check. When Willow departed, I snuck the muffin out of my sack, and the doggie cookie, even though Sushi had already had one. I knew she would demand it. Trying to reason with her did no more good than trying to reason with Mother.

Meanwhile, Jessica had not finished maligning the city council.

"The first thing I'd do," she was saying, "is replace the mayor with somebody who doesn't spend more time at that Indian casino than with that poor neglected wife of his. And next on the chopping block? Wally Thorp—he's *so* ineffectual, just always goes along with whatever the others want. Besides, I heard he's been running around on *his* wife."

"Yuck," said Amy. "Who'd want *him?*"

"Someone into balding, sloppy, overweight men, apparently."

"Who would *that* be?"

"*That* much info I *don't* have." Jessica, leaning in, went on: "And Lottie Everhart? *She* can go—mean, those slutty dresses! I don't think she cared a hoot about her husband's suicide—if it *was* a suicide."

"Oh, come on!" Amy said. "Mike killed himself over that Poe picture! Everybody knows that. But . . . what do you think about Paula Baxter?"

"Not much. Don't really know her, or much about her, either. Do you?"

Amy shrugged. "Seems to keep to herself."

I started in on the second muffin. No sense in returning with just one. Breakfast tomorrow was . . . breakfast tomorrow.

"Well," Amy was saying, "*Rick Wheeler* sure can stay—what a hunk! Wouldn't mind dating *him*."

Jessica snorted. "Well, good luck with *that*."

"What? He's fair game, isn't he? He's single."

"I hear Rick bats for the other team."

"You're crazy," Amy said.

Jessica shrugged. "That's what those gossips at the nail salon are saying. He was pretty tight with Mike, if you get my drift."

"Oh, you're terrible. They were just drinking buddies."

Customers were bunching up by the front door, waiting for a table, and I started to feel guilty about lingering over a now-empty glass and the crumbs of a muffin purchased (sort of) elsewhere. So I brushed the evidence off Sushi and me, left enough money to cover the tab and the tip, and got up.

Back out in the heat, I was debating where to go next when a voice called out, "*There* you are!"

Mother, still in full Poe regalia (mustache and all), was weaving through pedestrians on the sidewalk, getting raised eyebrows and "What the?" looks.

Planting herself in front of me, she proclaimed, "Deserted by my deputy! 'How sharper than a serpent's tooth it is to have a thankless child!' "

Shakespeare was always Mother's "go-to" when trying to shame me. Apparently Poe had never written anything about ungrateful offspring.

"I thought I ought to put Sushi out," I replied lamely. "How did you know I left? I was sitting back a ways—maybe you just didn't see me."

She threw back her head, her eyes rolling up. "I can see *plenty* without my glasses, when I have a mind to!"

Vivian Borne didn't see all that well when she *did* have her glasses on, otherwise maybe she wouldn't have racked up all those driving violations.

I shrugged. "You were almost done when I left."

"Oh, please! You were gone before I even *mentioned* Lenore!" She yanked off her mustache, causing another passerby to jump. "It may interest you to know that those who stayed for the duration gave me a *standing ovation* at the conclusion of my performance! In fact, I had barely finished when they began getting to their feet."

Only a thankless child would think, *Because she had* finally *finished*.

But I replied, "That's wonderful to hear. Sorry I missed the last few minutes." Time to change the subject. "I overheard some interesting dirt in the coffee shop."

"Concerning?"

"Antiqua's esteemed city council members. Some of it pretty steamy."

Her demeanor suddenly improved, eyes wide and sparkling now. "Ah! Tantalizing as that sounds, you'll have to share it with me later—I'm off to have an interview with the area media. Wish me luck. Maybe it'll make the AP!"

"Break a leg."

She eyed me suspiciously, as she always did when I gave her that traditional show biz advice, then she smiled and disappeared into the crowd.

I looked down at the panting shih tzu in my arms. "What do you say we go back to our air-conditioned Pullman?"

Sushi nodded again. (She did!)

I stepped into the flow of sidewalk traffic, letting it pull me along, but exiting at the first cross street to head in the direction of the Bed With No Breakfast, aka the Train That Went Nowhere.

My route took me by the white clapboard Heartland Church, with its sign advertising the Sunday sermon:

WHAT IS THE MEANING OF HELL?
THE CHOIR WILL BE SINGING.

I pondered that for a moment, then walked on.

Next to the church was a cemetery shaded by tall pine trees. Sushi squirmed, then barked, telling me she had something to do. So I left the sidewalk and put her down in a grassy spot away from any graves. But instead, the little scamp ran off through the tombstones. I couldn't blame her, the little darling having been cooped in either the SUV or the Pullman all day.

"Don't go very far!" I called out, then followed her into the cemetery.

A wind had kicked up, causing the boughs of the pines to sway. Their rustling leaves seemed to whisper to me—or was that the cemetery's dearly departed, offering a welcome . . . or warning?

The deeper I wandered into the graveyard, the older the headstones became. In a section where people had died in the mid-eighteen hundreds, epithets were the norm. Some were pretty standard—religious and/or inspirational—but some were humorous.

Here lies Daniel Tuke, the second fastest draw in Antiqua.

Mary Brown lived each day as if it were her last, especially this one.

Here rests Isaac Wigham, a big rock fell on his head.

Smedley Crisp's last words were "Watch this!"

I was trying to imagine what ill-conceived action Smedley Crisp might have taken, when I sensed a movement directly behind me and whirled, the way you do in a graveyard when a sound spooks you. Exactly the way.

"Didn't mean to startle you, young lady."

He was tall and thin, almost cadaverous, with cropped white hair. He wore a black suit, black shirt and shoes, and looked like an undertaker. But at least he'd called me "young."

"That's okay," I said, my heart still thumping.

"I'm Pastor Creed."

I introduced myself, including my kind-of-a-deputy status.

"I see," he said, "that you've been looking at the old Quaker gravestones."

"Yes. The Quakers seem to've had quite a sense of humor."

The pastor frowned. "Droll as those inscriptions may appear, I don't really believe that they did. Have a sense of humor."

Oh.

"Your church is Quaker?" I asked.

"Nondenominational, now." Something about that seemed regretful.

"And the cemetery? It belongs to the church?"

His response was a weight-of-the-world sigh that almost seemed too much for his slender shoulders. "We couldn't afford the financial upkeep, so the city took it over. Now *anyone* can be buried here."

There goes the neighborhood.

Pastor Creed cocked his head. "You plan to participate in the festival while you're in Antiqua?"

"Too crowded for me," I said, shaking my head.

He made a disgusted sound with his lips. "It'll only get worse, I'm afraid."

If you were looking to receive the light of God from this preacher, I doubted you'd need shades.

"You don't approve of the event?" I asked.

"I do not!" the pastor said. "Any idolatry of that man and his evil works is an offense to God."

"Poe, you mean?"

"Indeed."

"It does bring in business."

"No good can come from the work of the devil."

Oh-kay . . .

"But then," he said, apparently sensing my discomfort, his voice softening somewhat, "that's just my opinion . . . and I seem to be in the minority."

An awkward silence.

"Well," Pastor Creed said with a sigh, "I must work on my Sunday sermon. You're welcome to attend services, young lady. Ten o'clock—and the church is air-conditioned."

He found a smile for me, and I found one for him, saying, "Thank you, Pastor."

He nodded and headed back toward the church.

Sushi appeared at my feet.

"*There* you are," I said.

But as I bent to pick her up, she ran off through the tombstones again! And every time I got within a few feet of her, she scampered away.

"It's too *hot* to play!" I hollered.

Sushi kept the game up until she'd led me to a small stone mausoleum, where she sat suddenly down. That was odd. I thought she was looking for a place to piddle and suddenly she's Lassie leading me to the well that Timmy fell into.

The ancient structure was approximately ten by twelve feet and had a pyramidal roof. Grecian columns flanked a wooden door, above which was carved the name of the occupant—Henrietta Keller 1829–1911.

Why had Sushi brought me here?

Something glittered on the ground. I walked over and picked it up—a long, silver chain with a black raven pendant, wings spread.

Like the necklace Morella had worn.

I brought it up to my nose, and a sniff suggested the faintest scent of . . .

. . . Shalimar perfume.

I looked at the panting Sushi. Was *that* why she'd led me here? Had her nose led her to this necklace . . . ?

Two crumbling stone steps led to the mausoleum's door and an oxidized iron handle. I tried the handle and, to my astonishment, the door opened, flooding the windowless room with light, revealing a single unadorned stone sarcophagus at its center.

Around the periphery, spent cigarettes—marijuana, judging by the faint but noticeably sweet, floral scent—littered the concrete floor, indicating there had been other visitors here besides me, Sushi, and unlikely mourners.

I approached the sarcophagus and saw that the lid did not properly fit on its base. My eyes traveled to the floor, noting a fine ground powder created by stone scraping upon stone. The lid had been moved.

What I did next I can only say was instinctive.

Putting the heels of my hands against the rim of the lid, I pushed. And gritted my teeth and shoved some more, until, incrementally, the heavy top had dislodged enough for me to see within.

And there, on top of the bones presumably belonging to Henrietta Keller, lay a considerably younger woman and yet now as old as she'd ever be . . .

Morella, wearing a frozen, wide-eyed expression of terror more terrible than the grinning skull looking up past her.

A Trash 'n' Treasures Tip

When using the services of a book dealer, make sure he or she is qualified; for example, have they earned certification from the Antiquarian Booksellers' Association of America, or a similar organization, such as the International League of Antiquarian Booksellers? Just because a book dealer has some years on him or her, doesn't mean their merchandise is antique too. Or, as Mother says, "Don't judge a book by its cover—even if the leather is well-aged."

Chapter Three

Poe Blow

When Mother arrived on foot, summoned by my text, I was seated outside the mausoleum on its stone steps, holding Sushi protectively.

"Are you all right, dear?" she asked, out of breath, still in her Poe costume. At least her glasses were back on and the mustache a memory.

I nodded numbly.

"Where *is* the poor girl?"

I gestured with my head.

Mother entered the crypt, then—after a few minutes, which seemed like hours—returned to sit next to me, her knees cracking on the way down, the sound as if she were snapping her fingers.

"Took quite a blow to the head," Mother said, as if reporting we should pick up milk at the store. "Been in there awhile—rigor has come and gone. Perhaps we should call the authorities."

"Mother, you *are* the authorities."

Her eyes widened and she smiled big. "Why, so I am! I forgot for a moment—this is my first murder on the job, after all. My first look through the official telescope! Now, I must remember my training."

Training from 160 hours of night classes at the community college, qualifying her to be sheriff. Barely. Of course her amateur standing was second to none. . . .

I said, "I believe, as county sheriff, you have Serenity's police forensics department at your disposal. . . ."

"I know that," she replied defensively.

"Just trying to help."

"Of course, dear." She made the call.

Then she smiled at me apologetically. "Don't mean to be short with you. It's just the darn heat. Now, before I call the lab boys in . . ." She paused for a moment, relishing what she'd just said. "Tell me, how is it you know the girl?"

"I don't, really," I said. "She was a waitress at the coffee shop. Took my order yesterday. Her first name is Morella—no idea what her last is, but that would be easy enough to find out."

"And how did you happen to find her here?"

I filled Mother in on how Sushi had done the detecting.

She patted Sushi's head. "Good girl. I always *thought* you were part bloodhound!"

Sushi just gave her a look.

Mother put a finger to her cheek and squinted into her thoughts. "Shalimar on the necklace, you say? Interesting choice of fragrance—too heavy for my tastes. I prefer something lighter, with hints of black currant buds and lily of the valley . . . like Anaïs Anaïs or Eau de Charlotte."

I stared at her. "*Must* you be so insensitive? A young woman has been murdered!"

Now Mother gave me a look, eerily like the one Sushi had given her. "I *know* that, dear. But the best way I can help her now . . . only *real* way we can help her now . . . is to put emotionalism aside and find the one who did this.

Perhaps the perfume holds significance—an expensive pur-chase for a mere waitress in a small town, don't you think? There may be a boyfriend lurking somewhere."

Mother might be guilty of spreading a trail of nonsense in her wake, but even before she'd become sheriff, she had a no-nonsense and frankly rather cold attitude toward death in general and murder in particular.

She got to her feet, using a hand on my noggin for sup-port, saying, "I'll call Deputy Chen and fill him in."

"Mind if I wait inside the church?" I asked.

"Excellent suggestion—you'd be out of everyone's way, yet still available for further questioning."

What was I, a suspect or a sort-of-deputy?

She raised a cautionary finger, as if about to start "The Raven" again. "But don't go mentioning details of the death to this Pastor, uh . . . what did you say his name was?"

"Creed."

"Pastor Creed . . . or anyone else, for that matter. For now, just say the late young lady was found inside the mau-soleum . . ."

Young lady. That was what the pastor had called me.

". . . but not specifically *where* within it. No mention yet of apparent death by blunt object. And yes, you can use her name. It will get out soon enough."

I nodded.

Mother produced her cell phone from the frock coat's pocket to take pictures, and I stood holding Sushi, who squirmed just a little, probably preferring to do her own traveling. But this was a crime scene, after all, so with the dog in my arms, I trudged toward the church, feeling as if I were walking on sand. Or maybe quicksand.

Parked near the back of the building was a red truck, bearing more than a few scrapes and dings, its open cargo area laden with red bricks. Two men in work clothes—one young, the other older—were pushing brick-filled wheel-barrows toward the old storm cellar entrance to the basement, like the one Dorothy tried to get into when the tornado came.

I walked around to the double front doors of the church, found them open, and entered, immediately disappointed that it was not cool inside. The air-conditioning must have been reserved for Sunday services only.

There was no vestibule, the sanctuary stretching out before me like an old one-room schoolhouse: wooden floor showing decades of wear; hard oak pews sans cushions; and plain, uncurtained windows. To my right, tethered to a hook on the wall, a rope led up to the small open tower, where a cast-iron bell waited patiently to summon sinners.

At the opposite end of the room was a wide, stagelike chancel, two steps running its length, leading up to an unadorned altar, above which hung a roughly carved cross. To the left was a podium, to the right a row of chairs for the choir, and behind the chairs an old stand-up piano.

Two closed doors banked either side of the chancel, one marked RESTROOM and the other OFFICE. Behind the latter I heard a slam, of a drawer shutting maybe—the man of the cloth at work, apparently.

I sat in a back pew on the center aisle, Sushi down on the seat next to me, then stared at the cross, trying not to think of anything.

How much time passed I couldn't tell you—half an hour maybe—but after a while the door to the office opened, and Pastor Creed came out and headed up the outside aisle.

He didn't notice me at first, but then stopped short. "Miss Borne!"

"Didn't mean to startle *you*, this time."

He found a fold of a smile. "Turnabout's fair play, they

say. We don't get many visitors in the midafternoon, even when Antiqua's full of tourists."

He edged through the pew to reach me, then paused, eyes briefly taking in Sushi before returning to mine, apparently deciding not to complain about the canine parishioner.

"You look upset, child," he said.

Was that a promotion or demotion from "young lady," I wondered.

I told him how I'd discovered Morella in the mausoleum and that Mother was on the scene and other authorities were on the way.

On an exhale, the pastor said, "Dear Lord."

He sat next to me, then bowed his head and folded his hands in his lap. His lips moved in silent prayer.

When he had finished, Creed said resignedly, "And yet . . . I'm not surprised."

"Pardon?"

"I would imagine a drug overdose."

"What?"

"Was the cause of it. Isn't that the case?"

"I wouldn't know. I just found her. I'm not the coroner."

That was a little snippy, but he didn't seem to notice. He explained himself, quietly. "Seems I'm always finding evidence of drug use in that particular mausoleum. I've told the city council about it, repeatedly. Asked the mayor personally to put a secure bolt on the door." He sighed. "But nothing has been done. Perhaps they'll do something now."

"Did you know Morella?"

"Not really, no. Certainly not well. I know she works . . . worked at the coffee shop, and I'd seen her around town at times with a sketchy crowd."

"Was she part of your congregation?"

He shook his head. "She never attended services. Not even Christmas or Easter. Of course, most of the youth in this town aren't exactly devout. Just look at the way they dress! How they mutilate themselves with hedonistic tattoos and piercings."

I shrugged. "A lot of them wear crosses, though."

From below us came a loud noise, like rocks being broken by a sledgehammer. I jumped a little, though Pastor Creed seemed barely to notice.

"Sorry," the pastor said with a faint smile. "The workmen are replacing a buckling wall." Then, with a more distinct frown, he said, "Perhaps I should go see if I can be of any help."

"I don't think you should."

"Oh?"

Through the window onto the parking lot, I could see a white utility van pulling up to the cemetery entrance.

"The forensics officers are here," I said, "and they won't be wanting anyone near the mausoleum except the sheriff."

"Forensics?" the pastor said with alarm. "Why would *they* be called? Won't an autopsy confirm an overdose?"

"It would, if you're right about that," I replied, keeping the blunt object information to myself as Mother had instructed. "Sheriff Borne is just being thorough, and besides, forensics is part of Antiqua's contract whenever there's a . . ." I hesitated to say "suspicious." "An unexpected death."

He seemed to accept that, saying, "Then I will take the opportunity to pray for that poor girl's soul. Perhaps our Lord God will be lenient and consign her not to Hell but the mercy of Purgatory."

Not exactly my idea of mercy, but different strokes.

The pastor stood, stepped past me into the aisle, then walked down to the elevated chancel, where he approached the altar, knelt before the cross, and once again bowed his head.

The church doors opened and a blast of hot air entered, as if God Himself had decided to deliver the pastor a prompt reply. But it was only the still-Poe-clad Mother. She came over quickly, and I moved down so she could plop herself next to me. I could almost smell her burning.

Ignoring the tail-wagging Sushi, Mother said through clenched teeth, "How *dare* they tell *me* to vamoose! I'm the *sheriff!* And yet I get no respect!"

Her and Rodney Dangerfield.

I said dryly, "Maybe it's the costume."

"I haven't had *time* to change," she snapped.

"At least you removed the mustache. But maybe the wig should go too."

She looked more like the fake Paul McCartney in a Beatles tribute band than Edgar Allan.

With a glare, she yanked off the wig and tossed it on the other side of me. Sushi glanced at it as if wondering whether to growl. Mother, her hair in a bun but askew here and there, tendrils doing a modest Medusa-like thing, had not really improved the situation.

"And aren't you hot in that coat?" I asked.

"No. I adapt to all manner of weather. But I admit it is cumbersome. And my deodorant is really getting a workout."

"You're telling me."

"Don't be unkind, dear. This is the Lord's house."

The coat came off too and got tossed on top of the wig.

Meanwhile Mother's eyes went questioningly to Pastor Creed at the altar.

"He's arbitrating," I informed her, "on behalf of Morella's soul."

"Good for him," she said condescendingly.

The doors opened again, and Mayor Myron Hatcher

strode in, his face red and sweating, eyeglasses steamed over, shirt as drenched as if from a downpour.

Behind Myron came his fellow city council members— Paula Baxter, Lottie Everhart, Wally Thorp, and Rick Wheeler.

The group gathered at the mouth of our pew, glancing around at one another as if wondering who had the collection plate.

Finally the mayor said, "Sheriff, how is the death of this girl going to impact our festival?"

Standing next to the mayor, dark-haired, attractive Lottie looked daggers at him. "That *would* be your chief concern!"

"We'll have no infighting," Mother said sharply, a teacher to an unruly class. She motioned to the pew in front of her. "Now, sit down so I don't have to crane my neck."

They entered the designated pew, first Wally, then Paula, Rick, Lottie, and Myron. They sat themselves, then twisted to look back at Mother. Let them crane *their* necks.

"The mayor's question is a valid one," Mother told them. "Although it could have been presented with more tact and compassion."

Look who was talking.

Nonetheless, Myron apologized. "I meant no disrespect to the deceased young woman. But this is a vital weekend to our community. A lot is riding on it."

Paula, the redheaded, fiftyish owner of Relics Antiques, asked, "What exactly *happened*, Sheriff? Myron said you called him saying Morella has been found dead in the church cemetery and that we all should come over here. Was she in the mausoleum? Is *that* why those men are in there?"

"Correct," Mother said. "Brandy here, my deputy daughter, discovered her."

That rather sounded like I was her daughter's deputy, and I could tell several of the council members were trying to process that. I gave them no help.

Mother went on quickly, "Who can tell me something about this young woman? Do you know if she has family in town, or elsewhere for that matter?"

The group looked blankly at one another.

"Anyone?" Mother pressed. "Shall we begin with her last name?"

Rick, the council's resident hunk, shrugged one shoulder. "Her last name's Crafton. I didn't really know her at all. Other than that she worked at the coffee shop. And didn't love living here."

Paula said, "I never even go *in* that coffee shop—the prices are outrageous! Do they imagine they're Starbucks? But I *have* seen Morella around."

"She's waited on me a few times," Myron said. "But we've never exchanged anything more than idle chitchat." He frowned. "I *do* think Morella was new in town— maybe here a few years? But I don't remember whether she told me that or I heard it from someone. Anyway, she was not terribly friendly."

Lottie was nodding. "Rather sullen, I'd say. Honestly, I don't know *what* she was doing here. Why would she move here when she *hated* the place?" She looked down the line at Wally, who was sitting at the end. "Doesn't Morella rent the apartment above your shop?"

The group was having trouble with whether to discuss the dead girl in present or past tense. That was hardly unusual, but having found her, I knew past tense applied.

Pudgy, balding Wally, whose face looked rather puffy, said, "Yes, but she had her own entrance in back of the building. I never saw her come and go. I mean, really, she was just a tenant."

Mother said, "Surely you had conversations with her when she paid the rent, at least."

Wally shook his head, and it was unclear whether that was in sadness or just a gesture that said no.

"Morella really wasn't very friendly," he said with a slow shrug. "She'd just pass me an envelope with the rent money in it, first of the month, and nod and go off. But on the other hand? She didn't cause any trouble, either."

During this exchange, Pastor Creed had joined us, taking a seat in the pew across the aisle.

Mother addressed him: "Pastor? Do *you* have anything to add about Morella?"

He shook his head. "She was not a member of this church."

"And yet presumably one of God's children," Mother said with false cheer. "Nothing else you might have to say about her? It's a small community, Pastor."

Mother waited for more, but when nothing came but a single head shake, she returned her attention to the others. "Where were each of you last night?"

The immediate response was an almost comic array of startled expressions.

"Why on earth do you ask?" the mayor asked. "Surely this was an overdose! Everyone in *town* knows what that mausoleum is used for."

"And yet," Pastor Creed said, "none of you have done anything about it, despite my pleas."

Ignoring him, the mayor went on, "I can't possibly see how what any of us were doing last night would have any bearing on that girl's sad demise."

"But it might," Mother said. "Let's say you were out and about during the late evening hours and happened to see Morella walking in the cemetery, or noticed some other activity there. *That* would be helpful, wouldn't you say?"

Have I mentioned that Mother could be very sneaky?

"Well, yes," Myron agreed, nodding. "I was at my shop all evening, until well after midnight—getting ready for the festival this morning, of course. But my route home afterward did *not* take me by the church and the cemetery."

Mother's eyes went to Lottie.

Prompted, the sexy widow said, "I was in the Happy Hour bar all evening with some girlfriends. We left about . . . oh, eleven-thirty. And I did *not* go home by way of the cemetery, either."

Lottie turned her head to look at Rick. "You were there, too, at the Happy Hour."

He nodded, shrugged. "Not much else to do in this town. I went home about midnight. My route home doesn't take me by here either."

Paula was next in line. "I took a sleeping pill and went to bed early, about nine. After that I was dead to the world . . . sorry. Not appropriate."

Wally came last. "I watched a movie with my wife," he said. "Then she went to bed, and I fell asleep in my chair, stayed there all night."

Mother didn't seem to be interested in the pastor's whereabouts.

"Getting back to Edgar Allan Poe Days," Myron said, adding with a tinge of sarcasm, "if *now* is an okay time . . . I'm concerned about how this . . . development . . . is going to affect the event." He looked at Mother. "Can you guarantee to keep this news away from the public for a few days?"

Mother's cheeks flushed. "No, mayor, I *can't.* But the woman's identity will be withheld until her next of kin is notified, of course." She raised a finger. "But these things have a way of getting out. And I will be asking questions around town . . . and of course will do my best to do so discreetly."

Discretion did not come easily to Mother. It would be interesting to see if her role of sheriff changed that.

"Thank you," Myron replied. "And I'm sorry if I sounded insensitive about the girl's death. Obviously this is a tragedy. It's just . . . we depend on this festival to keep Antiqua afloat."

If the mayor was looking for absolution, he didn't get it from Mother, even if we were in church.

"Are you finished, Sheriff?" Paula asked. "We all need to get back to our stores."

"Finished for now," Mother said pleasantly.

The council members exchanged wary looks, then stood and exited, bunched together but for Wally, who trailed after.

Mother and I extricated ourselves from the pew, Sushi again in my arms. Pastor Creed also stood, then met us in the aisle.

"You didn't ask me where *I* was last night, Sheriff," he said. "But, for your information, I was in the parsonage all night and didn't notice any activity in the cemetery."

"Thank you, Pastor," Mother replied. "Were you alone?"

"Uh, yes. Certainly."

"You're unmarried?"

"I am."

An awkward silence.

No one had to say that his alibi was worthless or that his proximity to the cemetery made him a good suspect. Not to mention his contempt for the late girl. Though, I guess I did mention it. . . .

"Well," the man of God said, with a nervous smile, "I have the Sunday service's bulletin to prepare—if you'll excuse me."

"Certainly," Mother said with a nod.

"May I, uh . . . make a suggestion?"

"Yes?"

He nodded toward her black vintage suit of clothes. "If you have a uniform, I'd put it on. That wardrobe is distracting, and not in a good way."

Mother nodded again. "I'll take it under advisement."

As he headed back to his office, I whispered, "If I'm the one giving you advisement, I have to say I agree with him."

"Noted."

"But don't discount him, Mother. He was pretty clear to me about his dislike of the celebration of Poe. And the use of that mausoleum. And Morella's lifestyle."

"Noted."

I went on: "And there's a waitress named Willow at the coffee shop who worked with Morella. You should talk to her."

If she said "Noted" again, I was going to kick her in the sanctuary.

But instead she said, "Most helpful, dear."

Outside the church, we paused on the steps and looked across to the cemetery, where the forensics officers were diligently carrying on their work inside and outside the mausoleum. Nearby, an ambulance waited to transport Morella's remains back to Serenity for autopsy.

I said, "Sushi and I are going back to the Pullman."

Mother turned to me. "Yes, dear, have a nice lie-down. You look dreadful."

"Thank you."

Mother held out her coat and wig, then dug her mustache out of a pocket. She handed all of the junk to me.

"Will you take these back, dear? I'll join you in a while, but first I must speak to the officers. I don't want any attention-drawing crime scene tape used, so they must complete their work this afternoon. We'll want to withhold the cause of death awhile longer."

I shifted Sushi to one hand, the wardrobe items in the

other. And off I trudged, a migraine building up steam in my head.

Back in the Pullman, the cool air that greeted me felt good—at first. But then my stomach lurched, and I dropped Mother's costume onto the couch, and Sushi on top of them, then bolted for the bathroom, where I hunched over the toilet and lost what remained of the muffins and latte.

Done retching, I rinsed out my mouth, took some migraine medication, ran cold water on a washcloth, headed to the bed, got under the covers, and put the folded wet cloth across my eyes.

Sushi joined me, curling up by my side.

My cell phone, which I'd placed on the nightstand, vibrated.

I removed the cloth and checked the caller.

Tony Cassato, Serenity's chief of police, my on-again, off-again, and now on-again boyfriend.

"Are you all right?" he asked, the concern in his voice obvious.

I wanted to cry, but I knew that would only make my head throb more.

"I'm okay," I lied.

"I understand you found the body."

"Yes. Not very pleasant."

"I could be in Antiqua in under an hour."

"No. I'm in bed with a migraine, and plan to stay there."

"Okay. But if you change your mind . . ."

"Could you come Saturday night?"

"I'll make that happen. Get some sleep. How . . . how is your mother doing with this thing?"

"Surprisingly well, actually."

His laugh was a grunt. Or maybe his grunt was a laugh.

He said, "Not like it's her first murder case," and we said our good-byes.

I drifted off for a while, then awoke to find Mother, dressed in her jumpsuit uniform, perched on the edge of the bed.

"Feeling better, dear?" she asked.

The migraine had receded, and I burst into tears, sobs racking my body, scaring Sushi off the bed.

"There, there," Mother soothed. "This too shall pass."

I wasn't able to take finding a murder victim as lightly as Mother could . . . though that wasn't fair, was it? She just had a realistic view of human mortality—for all her theatrical ways, she had a down-to-earth take on death.

When I was able to speak, I asked, "She . . . she wasn't *dead* when someone put her in there, was she?"

"No, dear."

"Her nails . . . they were broken and bloody."

Mother nodded. "And her face had a blue cast—a telltale sign of asphyxia."

I managed to sit up. "Who would *do* such an evil thing?"

Mother shook her head, her expression grave. "I don't know, but I will certainly find out. Antiqua needs to know there's a new sheriff in town."

That made me laugh through the tears, though Mother just looked at me curiously.

Sushi jumped back up and lay down at the bottom of the bed.

Mother, eyes narrowed, said, "The killer probably thought Morella was dead when he or she put the poor child inside the sarcophagus. She'd already taken that blow to the head."

"So he's just a killer," I said, annoyed, "and not a sadist? How is that better?"

"Dear, I'm not defending this person. I merely mean we are dealing with someone driven to violence, with a motive. Not who kills for the sheer fun of it."

That gave me a shiver. "I know."

We fell silent for a few moments.

Then Mother said, "Tell me what you overheard at the coffee shop about the council members."

Not quite feeling up to giving her chapter and verse, I said, "Myron may have a gambling problem, Rick seems to be interested in men, Paula has no friends, Wally Thorp has a woman on the side, and Lottie wasn't all that broken up about her husband's suicide."

Mother's eyes sparkled behind the large glasses she was now wearing again. "Lovely concise answer, dear! And most interesting. *Especially* Wally. He seemed the most upset about Morella's death—did you notice?"

"He was pretty quiet," I agreed. "Awfully pale. But, Morella with *Wally?* That seems far-fetched."

Mother raised an eyebrow. "People are attracted to people for all kinds of reasons."

Something that had been in the back of my mind jumped to the fore.

"Mother, the necklace. . . ."

"What about it, dear?"

"The clasp wasn't broken."

She frowned. "I don't follow."

"Think it through."

"Oh, I see where you're coming from! If Morella had wanted to leave the necklace for someone to find, she would have torn it from her neck and dropped it."

"Otherwise," I said, "if the necklace had *accidentally* been ripped off, the clasp would have been broken as well."

Mother was nodding. "The killer removed the necklace and left it outside the mausoleum *purposely.*"

"But why?"

"So she would be found *sooner*, dear."

"To close down the festival?"

Mother frowned. "There's another possibility."

"What's that?"

Her eyebrows were high. "Does the *manner* of Morella's death remind you of anything?"

A chill ran up my spine, and my eyebrows climbed, too. "Poe's 'Premature Burial'!"

"'Premature' precisely!" Mother stood and gazed down at me, troubled. "Dear, what would you say if I suggested we might have an Edgar Allan Poe copycat in our midst?"

". . . That maybe our killer is a sadist after all?"

She nodded. "As well as quite mad."

A Trash 'n' Treasures Tip

Many online book sites allow you to list with them the rare books you are searching for. Using several sites at once will save time, and give you the best price. There's usually a limit of titles you can list, however. The two hundred volumes Mother is looking for had to be spread around some.

Chapter Four

Mother on the Poe

Dearest ones!

This is Sheriff Vivian Borne (that has a nice ring, don't you think?), assuming the narrative from Brandy, who has taken to her bed after the shock of discovering a corpse in a crypt (also a nice ring, if a bit bone-chilling).

Poor darling—Brandy, I mean, although that also might apply to the late Morella, a waitress who waits no more. (Poe worthy, no?) I'm afraid she (Brandy, again) lacks the strong, resilient constitution with which I have been blessed, allowing me to press on solo with the investigation, unhampered by my well-meaning but unimaginative pro bono deputy.

(**Brandy to Mother:** I *do* read these chapters of yours, you know. And in answer to your question a few lines ago? No.)

(**Mother to Brandy:** What question, dear?)

(**Brandy to Mother:** That *wasn't* Poe worthy. Call it a Poe attempt.)

But before I press on, I must address an issue having to do with my campaign for sheriff. I had received quite a

few donations from our overseas Trash 'n' Treasures readers, supporting my bid, and because there are stipulations
(unknown by me at the time) regarding a political campaign accepting foreign money, I feel it necessary to return
those donations, to maintain transparency and stay above-
board. (There's always the possibility that Russia may
have routed me rubles through fictitious names, hoping to
tip the scales in my favor—but rectifying this is beyond
even Vivian Borne. *Spasiba*, though!)

So, if you live outside the good old US of A and have
sent me money, expect reimbursement soon. After cur-
rency exchange, there is $37.87 that must, in all good con-
science, be returned.

I also need some help with a small cardboard box I received containing *stotinki* coins. I didn't even *know* our
books were available in Bulgaria! Anyhoo, the return address was missing, so I don't know who sent it. If you are
the Bulgarian party (person, not political group), would
you please drop me a note or e-mail, or contact our publisher, and identify how many *stotinki* were in the box so
that I know it is really you?

Thank you in advance.

And now back to our story.

After leaving Brandy and Sushi behind in our Pullman
car, I decided to trek over to the Coffee Club and speak to
Willow, the waitress Brandy mentioned.

Approaching six p.m., the sidewalks were not nearly as
crowded as before. The shops were closed for the day,
folks either at the Antique Diner having dinner or at the
Happy Hour bar drinking, else back at their lodgings or
heading home to nearby towns.

As I stepped inside, a young woman sweeping the floor
said, without looking up, "We're closing."

Then she noticed my uniform with badge, and her dis-
position improved somewhat. "Oh . . . you must the new

sheriff. I guess I can still get you something—if it's not too complicated."

I shut the door behind me and approached the waitress, who was almost startlingly thin—a wisp of a willow, one might say. She wore a sleeveless white shirt and black jeans, her long brown hair in a ponytail. Hiding behind the heavy makeup was a pretty face.

"You're Willow?" I asked.

"Yes."

"I'd like a word—or two."

Her eyes widened. "What about?"

"Your late colleague, dear."

"My what?"

"Morella."

Sullen again, Willow leaned on the broom. "If you're looking for her, I don't know where she is, but she isn't just late—she didn't show at all! Tell her thanks a lot for sticking me with her shift, if you find her."

"Oh, she's been found," I said.

Willow's sculpted eyebrows rose. "What do you mean?"

"She's quite dead, dear."

I watched carefully for the young woman's reaction.

Willow took a few steps back, bumped into a chair, then dropped into it. The waitress stared at the floor, then looked up at me. "God. What . . . what *happened?*"

"Morella was discovered this afternoon in the mausoleum at the cemetery. Cause of death has yet to be determined, but others have suggested it might be the result of a drug overdose."

That was accurate, wasn't it? Others *had* suggested that.

Willow's ponytail switched back and forth, like a horse tail batting away flies. "No *way*. She didn't do drugs!"

"You're certain?" Even though I knew the late young woman had died from an overdose of blunt object, any information regarding her possible use of illegal substances might be helpful.

"I know she didn't because . . . ah . . ." The young woman halted, eyes drifting to my five-pointed star badge.

I pulled a chair out from the table and sat. "Young lady, you may rest assured that I'm not interested in your various peccadilloes."

"Pick a what?"

"Let's call them . . . bad habits."

"Oh. Okay. Well, then, the reason I know was because we got into it over that."

"Over what?"

"Over what kind of . . . recreational 'habits' were okay and what weren't. But that's all I'm gonna say on that subject."

"Understood," I said with a nod. "Did she have a paramour?"

"A pair of what? You sure talk funny for a sheriff."

"Did Morella have a boyfriend or lover?"

The waitress hesitated before answering. "No. Morella thought all the guys around here were losers. Not that she was wrong."

"Did she ever mention going out with anyone? Dating at all? Perhaps it came up in the midst of girl talk."

Willow waved a slender hand. "We didn't talk about girls *or* guys. Never had those kind of talks—we weren't close friends. All I know about her is, she showed up in Antiqua a couple years ago, got a job here, hated this town, and all she ever talked about was leaving it."

"When did you last see Morella?"

Willow thought for a moment. "Thursday morning, I guess. Yeah. Thursday morning. I stopped in here to remind her she was working for me this weekend so I could go to the festival."

"How did she seem?"

"Funny you should ask."

"Funny, dear?"

Willow shrugged. "She looked *happy*, for a change."

"Any idea why?"

A shrug. "Maybe she thought she finally found a way out of this town."

And hadn't she?

I asked, "Would you happen to know what Morella liked to do in her spare time?"

"Well . . . I know she went to the casino a lot—the Indian one? Now and then she said she won a little. Never talked about losing . . . but who does? It's no wonder she could never save enough to get out of this place, throwing her paycheck away like that all the time."

"I understand she lived in an apartment in town," I said, already knowing the answer.

Willow nodded. "Over that junk shop. And she drove an old blue Toyota. But, really, that's all I can tell you about her. I feel bad she's gone, but we weren't close, so . . . anyway. I have to finish cleaning up or I'll get my butt in a sling."

"Well, we can't have that, dear. Sounds most uncomfortable. Thank you for your time."

As I was heading toward the door, Willow called out, "Oh . . . Sheriff!"

I turned. "Yes?"

"Thursday morning? When I last saw Morella? Now that I think of it, she did say something . . . something kinda strange."

"What would that be, dear?"

"Some weird thing about a book cover."

"Could you be more specific? Exact words, Willow."

The sculpted eyebrows knitted together. "Ah . . . I think it was, 'Turns out you *can* judge a book by its cover.'"

"Interesting. Thank you. And might I offer a suggestion?

If you were to smile more, your inner loveliness would shine through."

"Huh?"

I left her to ponder that.

The sun hung low (for some reason, I'm craving Chinese food as I write this!) as I headed over to Junk 'n' Stuff, housed in a rather decrepit two-story building at the end of Antiques Drive. A CLOSED sign drooped from a nail on the front door, so I walked around back, where a blue Toyota, sporting more than its share of dents, was parked next to a flight of wooden steps to the second floor.

I climbed to the door, plucked a pair of lock picks from my duty belt, and in two shakes of Sushi's tail was inside. If you're wondering, I had probable cause—Morella, the occupant (former occupant now), had been murdered, after all.

It was pitch black within, so I used my small flashlight to locate a lamp and turn it on. I found myself in a living room with a worn carpet, inexpensive secondhandish furniture, and an old tube television. Empty beer cans littered a coffee table, along with an ashtray full of cigarettes butts.

The living room flowed into a small kitchen with low-end appliances, a sink full of dirty dishes, and a trash can containing pizza boxes and frozen food packaging.

A small hallway led to the only bedroom, where a suitcase, partially filled with feminine apparel, lay open on the unmade bed—apparently Morella had indeed been preparing to leave Antiqua.

I walked over to a scuffed-up four-drawer dresser, atop which a black purse sat, and proceeded to empty the bag's contents: wallet with driver's license, perhaps forty dollars in cash, and a bank debit card. I also found a single key for the car, but nothing that might fit the front door. Also M.I.A. was a cell phone, nor did I spot one lying around. I returned the items to the purse.

So.

Morella had left the apartment, taking along only her latch key and cell phone, then proceeded to the cemetery on foot.

A pile of papers on the floor drew my attention, and I picked them up, then found a spot on the bed to spread them out: paid bills, paycheck stubs, and statements from the local bank. Examining the latter—the bank still using photostats of checks and deposits—I noticed that Morella had been depositing two hundred dollars in cash every Friday, in addition to her paycheck.

Who or what had been supplementing her income? I very much doubted it was casino winnings.

My back was to the bedroom door when a voice boomed behind me: "What the hell are you doing?"

Reflexively, I twisted in that direction, doing my sacroiliac no favors.

"My *job*, Mr. Thorp."

The junk shop proprietor sighed. "You could have asked me for a key," he said tersely.

I stood, somewhat painfully. My first in-the-line-of-duty injury, or ache anyway. "How long has Morella been your tenant?"

He shrugged, irritated. "A couple years. I overheard her at the coffee shop saying she was looking for an apartment."

"And this happened to be vacant?"

"Not exactly," he said.

I waited for an explanation.

"This floor was just storage."

"Ah."

Wally gestured with an open, stubby-finger hand. "Morella was living in her car, and, well . . . I felt sorry for the kid."

I said, "A considerable outlay of cash, I'd say, to fix this place up for a stranger."

He bristled. "Business has been tough. I thought a rental could bring in income. And I had plenty of stuff downstairs I could furnish it with."

I asked, "And *has* it brought in more income? Did Morella pay her rent on time?"

A long pause. Another shrug. "She'd fallen behind."

"A bit behind, or . . . ?"

He swallowed thickly. "Four months."

I approached the man, recalling the rumor about his love interest on the side. "You're a very considerate land-lord, Mr. Thorp. Did you offer to work things out with her in some other way? Barter system, perhaps?"

Wally's eyes narrowed. "I don't think I like what you're implying."

It was my turn to shrug, which I did with dramatic flair. "I'm merely asking if perhaps Morella ever worked for you in your shop, to help pay off the debt. Sweeping up, that kind of thing."

"Oh. No. Stella—the wife? She comes in and does that every so often."

The wife. Such a charming way to put it.

"Earlier, at the church," I said, "you appeared upset about the young woman's demise . . . more so than the other council members, I would say."

"She was my *tenant*," he said, defensively.

I nodded. "Meaning a loss of income . . . at least, had she ever paid her back rent. Or perhaps you two had grown close—in a platonic way, of course—what with her living above the shop."

His chin tightened and crinkled. "Like I told you at the church, Mrs. Borne, that kid and me, we didn't have much contact."

"Did you ever notice your tenant entertaining any visitors? Girlfriends, perhaps? Boyfriends?"

He shook his head, rather more than the question might require. "No. After I close the store, I go home."

We had reached the point where Wally had given me all he was likely to.

So I said, "Well, thank you, Mr. Thorp. I'll make sure the apartment is locked up good and tight when I leave."

He hesitated a moment, then left the bedroom. I listened for the front door to open, and close. I gathered up the papers, took the purse, and left.

On Heirloom Drive, a side street, was a small Wells Fargo branch bank in a newish one-story red-brick building, not yet closed for the day. I entered the tiny lobby with its handful of comfy chairs, table with magazines, and side table with coffeemaker, pot empty. Straight ahead was a teller stationed behind a wooden partition.

I proceeded to the customer window. The young woman, barely out of her teens, frowned at my uniform and said, "Ah . . . we're about to close." The child was anxious, I would imagine, to escape her cage and get on with her young life. Particularly on a Friday.

"Tell your manager," I said pleasantly, "that Sheriff Borne needs a word."

She blinked, processing that. "Oh. Okay."

The teller disappeared through a doorway behind her, then came back to her post. "Ms. Gooch will be with you in a moment."

Soon a thirtyish, plump, rather plain-looking woman in a pink pantsuit came around the station and approached me. An unkind commentator might call her dumpy.

"Gladys Gooch," she said. "How might I help you, Sheriff?"

"Official business," I replied. "Could we talk in your office?"

"Certainly."

I followed Ms. Gooch around the partition and through the door into a small office.

Absorbing the room instantly, looking for leverage, I found it among the paperwork on her desk: a folded-open romance novel.

Gladys lowered herself into a swivel chair; I took the one for the client, which didn't swivel (the chair, not yours truly).

"I need information about Morella Crafton's checking account," I said with authority and a smile. "Specifically, I'd like the source of the two hundred dollars in cash she deposited every week."

The manager shook her head. "That would be impossible to know, since it *was* cash."

I asked, "Can't you cross-check it with withdrawals for that amount from other accounts?"

"Not really," she said, adding, "and even if I could, I wouldn't attempt such a search without a court order."

"Say that again," I said, putting some excitement into my voice.

"Huh?"

"About the court order!"

Gladys frowned, puzzled. "I wouldn't attempt such a search without a court order."

I put a hand to my bosom. "What a *voice* you have, my dear! Your annunciation, your projection. Have you ever trod the boards?"

"Trod on what boards?"

"The *stage*, dear! That's an expression meaning that one has performed as an actor. In public."

She smiled and some color came to her cheeks; it helped a little. "Oh. No. Well, a *little*, in high school. Just a tiny part."

I sighed deeply. "What a loss for the world of dramaturgy."

"You really think so?"

Sitting forward, I asked, "Are you aware of the semi-professional productions we've presented at the Serenity Playhouse?"

Her eyes were wide. "I've heard they're pretty good," she admitted.

"Well, although I am not here this afternoon in that capacity, I *am* executive director of the Playhouse."

I had a flash of inspiration (actually, I *enacted* a person who was experiencing a flash of inspiration).

"Ms. Gooch . . . how would you like to fill the lead role in *The Voice of the Turtle*?"

"The lead role is a . . . turtle?"

"No, dear!" I clasped my hands. "The role of Olive Lashbrooke, a worldly girl who lives, lives, lives! Whose unquenchable passions take her from one love affair to the next."

"Oh my." Ms. Gooch's eyes were quite wide now. "Do you really think I might have the . . . talent? To play her?"

"Why, you would be *perfect*." I batted away an invisible fly (mime training). "You wouldn't even have to audition. Your talent is palpable—it verily oozes from every pore."

"It does? Wow."

I sat back.

I waited.

Gladys sighed, sat forward. "Off the record?"

"Way off," I said.

The banker said conspiratorially, "I can tell you this much . . . Miss Crafton could have deposited a lot *more* than two hundred dollars every week. She always had a wad of cash that . . . you know the old expression, a roll of bills that would choke a horse?"

"I do indeed."

"Well, that's the kind of roll she'd peel that money off of."

"How much more than the two hundred she regularly deposited?"

The manager crinkled her nose. "Maybe *triple* that."

And yet Morella was four months behind in her rent. Interesting.

I rose and bowed. "Thank you, Gladys. I'll be in touch before we begin production in the fall."

She stood and gushed. "I can't believe it! Thank you. Could you send the script around?"

"You're welcome, and I certainly could provide you with the play. I'll see myself out."

I did not enjoy deceiving the woman—beyond the fun of it, of course—but I needed to solve Morella's murder by whatever means necessary. Besides, Gladys would probably forget all about the play.

(**Brandy to Mother:** So *that's* how Gladys Gooch got that part! "Oh, what a tangled web we weave when first we practise to deceive!" That's Shakespeare.)

(**Mother to Brandy:** Actually, Sir Walter Scott, darling child. And don't let's get ahead of ourselves—that's the *next* book.)

Night had fallen by the time I returned to the Pullman, its windows dark, Brandy apparently still slumbering. I fished a spare key to the Explorer from my duty belt, unlocked the vehicle, then slipped behind the wheel, placing the papers and purse on the seat next to me.

Carefully I backed out of the gravel drive, then (slowly at first) drove away. And, yes, I understand I am not allowed to drive as a civilian, but as a law enforcement professional, I have a right to commandeer a vehicle now and then. In an emergency. And in my book, "emergency" is a fluid term.

The Tomahawk—an off-reservation casino owned by

the Sauk (or Sac) Indians—was located among the corn-fields (or "maize") about ten miles west of Antiqua, just off the interstate. I had been to the gambling establishment once before, when it first opened, accompanied by few of my gal pals, seeking to try our luck with the one-armed bandits. After an hour, however, I became bored and laid my modest winnings down on the all-you-can-eat buffet, which turned out not to be a good bet.

The parking lot was almost full this evening, and finding a decent spot seemed impossible . . . until I remembered who I was, and parked my wheels at the curb near the front entrance.

I disembarked, then passed beneath an archway where a huge tomahawk was poised as if an indication that its patrons were about to be massacred. In the entryway, where the mosaic walls depicted pictorial American Indian scenes, stood a security guard in blue uniform. He had distinctly Indian features—high cheekbones, his dark hair pulled back in long braids—and reminded me of the Native American in that classic public service spot of decades ago, who cried at seeing garbage strewn across the landscape. Remember when commercials were fun?

"Sheriff Vivian Borne," I informed him. "Serenity County."

He raised a hand. "How—"

I raised mine, palm outward. *"How!"*

His eyes widened. "Uh . . . I was going to ask, 'How can I help you?'"

"Oh, I apologize," I replied. "I need a powwow with the top man on the totem pole."

(**Brandy to Mother:** You didn't really say that, did you?)

(**Mother to Brandy:** I was trying to speak his lingo.)

(**Brandy to Mother:** Well, that was offensive.)

(**Mother to Brandy:** I'm of another generation, dear,

and you will simply have to learn to leave your prejudice about my people behind. It's ageist.)

The security man, who for some reason was chuckling and shaking his head, walked over to a wall phone, and punched in numbers.

Shortly he returned and said, "Mr. Saukenuk will be right with you. He's the casino manager."

I thanked the guard, and stepped aside so he could return to scrutinizing incoming customers.

Before long, I was approached by a gentleman in his forties, smartly attired in a black suit, purple shirt, silver tie, and mirror-polished shoes. His blond, wavy hair was parted on the side, and his dark-framed glasses could not detract from the Paul Newman blue eyes.

"Sheriff Borne?" he asked. "Ben Saukenuk."

Reading my expression, he said with a little smile, "Not what you expected?"

"No," I admitted.

"I get that a lot. My great-grandfather was Sauk, but his wife was Swedish, and her genes had their way with great-granddad's offspring all down the line. Now, what can I do for you?"

When I told him I needed information on a casino patron who'd been here Thursday night, he suggested we talk in his office.

As we walked along a shiny, beige-tiled corridor, the casino manager filled the silence by asking, "Ever been to the Tomahawk before?"

"Once," I said, "before I became sheriff."

"I hope you enjoyed your experience."

"I made heap plenty wampum myself, but my girlfriends really got scalped."

(**Brandy to Mother:** Mother!)

(**Mother to Brandy:** The casino manager laughed. You need to lighten up.)

(**Brandy to Mother:** And *you* need sensitivity training.)

(**Mother to Brandy:** Do I? What about the usage of *moccasins* and *kayak*? Anything wrong with those? And did you know that the words *barbecue* and *caucus* come from American Indian languages? Are we to completely eradicate any vestige of the Native American's influence?)

(**Brandy to Mother:** I surrender, like Custer should have. *Cowabunga*, Mother.)

(**Mother to Brandy:** That's not from a Native American language, dear. It's from *Howdy Doody*.)

Ben Saukenuk escorted me into an executive office, its paneled walls arrayed with black-and-white photos of various Indian chiefs, their clothes and headwear becoming more modern with the passage of time.

He gestured to a padded chair in front of the desk. "Please take a seat."

I did.

"Can I interest you in a beverage?" Ben asked.

I declined the offer, and he settled in behind the desk. "Now, about this customer . . ."

"Morella Crafton." I handed him her driver's license, which I'd taken from the purse. "Do you know her?"

He studied the photo. "Can't say I do. But we have thousands of regulars. And I'm mostly stuck in this office. Let me bring in our floor manager." He reached for the phone on the desk.

While we waited, I admitted I knew very little about the Sauk Indian tribe, except that they lived on a small Indian reservation in adjoining Tama County and had their own law enforcement officers. Ben proceeded to enlighten me with a few other facts.

The Sauks had no chief. A tribal council, headed by a chairman, ran the reservation, which also had its own court system, public works, schools, medical facility, and bank. While the Sauk reservation was a little nation unto itself, it did work with area law enforcement and other outside entities as necessary. The tribe currently numbered about thirteen hundred.

The door opened and a man of indeterminate age entered—tall, beefy, and bald. He looked formidable, like a wrestler. His dark gray suit seemed barely able to contain his bulk. No one would give this man any trouble.

Ben said, "This is Jim Soaring Eagle, our floor manager. Jim, meet the new Serenity County sheriff, Vivian Borne."

Jim offered a hand the size of a catcher's mitt, and I shook it as best as I could.

"Jim," Ben said, holding out the driver's license, "do you know this woman?"

The floor manager took the card, studied it, then nodded and said in a deep growl of a voice, "I recognize her. She likes to play blackjack."

"Anything else?" I asked.

Jim looked at me. "No, just blackjack."

"I mean, can you tell us anything else about her?"

"Oh. Well . . . no. But you might check with Kimi Wanatee. The lady in this photo is usually at her table."

"Thank you, Jim," Ben said. "Kimi works most nights, doesn't she?"

"Yes. From six until midnight. She's here now."

"Find a substitute for her, please," Ben instructed. "And ask her to come to my office."

"Sure, boss. Nice to meet you, Sheriff."

"My pleasure," I said.

The floor manager left.

While passing time for the blackjack dealer to arrive, I learned more from Ben about the Sauk Indians, who originated along the St. Lawrence River in Ontario and northern New York state. Driven out by more powerful tribes, the Sauks migrated westward to the great lakes of Michigan, and then the fertile Mississippi Valley.

(**Note to Vivian from Editor:** While the aforementioned is interesting, does it have anything to do with the story?)

(**Note to Editor from Vivian:** Just trying to redeem myself a little here.)

The door opened and a beautiful young woman came in. She had exotic, almond-shaped eyes; a long, slender nose; a wide mouth with full red lips; and shoulder-length dark hair, shiny and straight. She wore a white long-sleeved shirt with black bowtie, vest, and slacks—standard for Tomahawk dealers.

Ben made the introductions, then showed Kimi the photo of Morella.

"Yes," the dealer said with a nod, "she's one of my regulars."

I asked, "Did Morella ever talk about herself?"

"No. We only exchanged a little polite conversation."

Ben said to me, "We discourage dealers from getting too familiar with the customers. For them it's recreation, but for us it's business."

I nodded, then looked at Kimi.

"There are quite a few blackjack dealers here. Why do you think Morella always wanted to be with you?"

Kimi considered my question, then replied, "I don't think it was me so much as, well . . . my other customers."

"Please explain," I said.

She shifted her stance, eyes going to Ben for help.

He again spoke for her. "Miss Wanatee is very popular among our high rollers."

With a smile, I said, "The male high rollers, I assume."

Kimi, a tad embarrassed, smiled and nodded. "The majority of high rollers are male."

"And," I asked, "Morella was attracted to such men?"

"Well," the attractive dealer said, "she certainly was very friendly with them . . . especially after a few drinks."

"Do you recall seeing her overdo any of that friend-liness?"

She shook her head, arcs of dark hair swinging. "No. Most players are deadly serious about the game and not interested in anything else. Now, if Morella ever met up with anyone afterward, I couldn't say. But she usually left before any of the others."

"Because she ran out of money?"

Kimi nodded. "Morella did generally lose." The dealer frowned. "Now, there *is* something odd. . . ."

"Yes?"

"She was here just the other night—"

"Thursday?"

"Yes. From about, oh, nine until ten or ten-thirty."

I nodded. "Go on."

"Well, for a change she was having a winning streak. Then she got a cell phone call. And I reminded her that if she answered it, she had to leave the game—casino policy."

"And?"

"She let it go to voice mail. But she bowed out anyway and left, which I didn't understand because, like I said, she was running hot."

Perhaps Morella had decided to quit before the tide turned.

I asked, "Any chance you saw the number?"

"No. She had the phone in her lap, under the table."

I gave her a smile. "Thank you, Kimi. That's all the time I need from you."

The dealer hesitated. "Is . . . is Morella in some kind of trouble?"

"No," I said.

Not any longer.

After the door closed behind Kimi, I told Ben I would like to see any surveillance footage of Morella Thursday night, and he agreed to provide it.

The surveillance area was in the bowels of the casino, and when Ben escorted me into the room, I remarked with surprise, "I was expecting something more substantial."

The operation was only a bit larger than Serenity's communications department.

I asked, "How can you possibly cover the entire casino?"

Ben, smiling patiently, explained, "Although there are only ten monitors manned by six employees, we have hundreds of cameras positioned throughout the casino and parking lot, and we can call up any of these cameras at any time. Since it's impossible to follow them all in real time, we rely on playback of the feeds and concentrate on certain areas."

"Which areas?" I asked.

He smiled a little. "The cashier cages, for instance. If someone is going to rip off the casino, it most likely will be an employee, or a customer stealing another patron's purse." He sighed. "You'd be surprised how dull a surveillance job can be."

"I understand," I said. "A lady reports her purse missing, and you find her on the playback and watch to see who took it, then follow that person out into the parking lot and get their license plate number."

"Yes. And that's about as exciting as it gets."

"What about card sharks and card counters?" I asked. "Are your employees trained to spot them?"

Ben shook his head. "That's the job of the pit bosses. When they see something suspicious, they notify surveillance, and we get a camera on the player, if one isn't. Then we watch the playback and take the appropriate action." He gestured with a hand. "Let's go over to the playback station."

I followed him to an area where a female in casual attire sat at a computer with large monitor. No introductions were made, but Ben told her what day, time, and area of the casino to bring up.

Soon Morella appeared on the screen, recorded from above.

I said, "I'm interested in the cell call she received."

The surveillance woman fast-forwarded the video, then stopped at the moment Morella reached into her pocket and withdrew her phone. The feed recorded the time as 10:26.

But the phone's screen was not visible.

I asked, "Is there another camera with a different angle?"

The technician replied, "I could check other cameras in that area, and zoom in, but it will take a little time. And the result will likely be very blurry."

"Contact me if you have any luck," I said. "I'd like to see the rest of the playback in real time, please."

I watched on various angles as Morella pocketed the phone, picked up her chips, left the table, and cashed the chips in at a cage. Then she walked out of the casino, got into her blue Toyota, and drove away.

During that time Morella spoke to no one, except to exchange a few words with the cashier. No one followed her out when she left.

I thanked the surveillance woman, and Ben walked me back as far as his office, where I thanked him. We shook hands and parted.

I decided to take a shortcut to the main entrance through the casino, and on my way I spotted a quarter on the carpet.

I had long been a believer in the old adage "See a penny, pick it up and all the day you'll have good luck." But due to my bad knees, I had upped that from a found penny to a quarter, so I stooped and retrieved the coin.

After spying a row of older coin-operated slot machines

with arms to pull, I put the quarter into one, pulled the lever, and walked on, certain that I wouldn't win one red cent—*excuse me!*—single penny.

But I was wrong. Was I *ever* wrong!

Sirens wailed and lights flashed as a rousing rendition of "Money (That's What I Want)" played, the cacophony of noise nearly sending me into an epileptic fit.

I had won $109,987.14!

Before I left, I was congratulated by Ben, who had me fill out some tax information before I arranged for the funds to be deposited in the First National Bank of Serenity.

When I arrived back at the Pullman, around one, I found the lights on, meaning Brandy was awake and waiting for me. I braced for a lecture.

Sure enough, the moment I stepped through the door, she started in. "Where have you been? Do you know what time it is? I was worried to death! Why didn't you call me? It was bad enough you turned your phone off." She paused for a breath. "And you should *never* have taken the car!"

Oddly, these were the same words I'd more than once spoken to Brandy when she was a teenager and sneaked out at night.

I waved a hand. "Not now, dear. We can have it out in the morning. I'm tuckered."

And I headed back to the bedroom.

My head had barely touched the pillow when I conked out, and it seemed like only a short time had passed before Brandy was shaking me awake.

"Let me have my coffee first, dear," I groaned. "Then we'll discuss my commandeering of the SUV and following up a lead at the casino."

"All of that will have to wait," Brandy said, her tone urgent.

I sat up on my elbows. "What's happened?"
"The mayor is missing."

Vivian's Trash 'n' Treasurers Tip

When a dealer finds the book you requested, be prepared to pay the asking price. If you are a regular customer, however, it is permissible to inquire about a discount—but don't expect much. (It's always helpful to have a little dirt on the person.)

Chapter Five

Poe Bono

Saturday morning, Mother and I downed a quick cup of coffee before leaving the Pullman at a little after eight. We headed to the mayor's home, which was about five miles south of town in the opposite direction of the interstate.

Behind the wheel of the Explorer, I said, "Maybe His Honor will have shown up by the time we get there."

Mother, recording our destination in the computer, replied, "That's not what my bones are saying, dear."

I'd only ever heard Mother's bones say "pop."

I turned left onto County Road G, where the flat farmland suddenly gave way to a forest of lush trees; after about a mile, I made a turn down a narrow, shade-tree-canopied gravel lane. And then, like Manderley in *Rebecca*, a mansion materialized out of the lingering morning haze.

Okay, so the Hatcher place wasn't anywhere close to the size of Manderley, or as venerable if almost as spooky; but for the residence of a mayor of a tiny town, the three-story Gothic revival limestone house, looking like an ancient church, made a pretty darn impressive abode.

I parked in the driveway behind a pristine burgundy Buick, and Mother and I exited.

Gazing up at the structure, she gave a long, low whistle. "Wonder what the history is of *this* cottage?"

Knowing Mother's fascination with antique homes, I warned, "Well, please don't get into that till you've conducted the interview. Remember why we're here. The owner is missing, remember?"

"I will not allow myself to be distracted, dear," she said, still looking up in wonder and stumbling on the first of nine stone steps to the stoop. Before we'd even rung the bell, a cathedral-style front door yawned open and the lady of the manor appeared, wringing her hands.

"Thank you for coming right out," Mrs. Hatcher said.

She was somewhere in her late fifties, tall, well-dressed in a pale blue pantsuit, her gray hair arranged in a short pageboy, her makeup slightly smeared from tears.

Mother clasped her hands together. "Any word of Myron?" she asked, working a little too hard to seem concerned. I knew that, in detective mode, she was about as sensitive as cast iron.

"Nothing," the woman said, shaking her head. She appeared dazed, framed there in the doorway, obviously lost as to what to do next. Mother took the initiative to brush past her and invite herself in.

I smiled sympathetically at our hostess and followed Mother.

Mrs. Hatcher closed the heavy door, then joined us in a large foyer, where it became necessary for the pro bono deputy to pick up the conversation.

Why?

Because the sheriff was staring openmouthed at the interior's grandeur, her eyes bugging behind her large lenses to bounce up the exquisitely carved staircase to the stained-glass windows on the landing, then down again and over to a huge, ornately carved grandfather clock, and up once more to a crown-like metal chandelier, which I hoped was securely attached to the ceiling, as we were all standing beneath it.

"Perhaps we should sit down?" I suggested, fighting memories of *Phantom of the Opera*.

Mrs. Hatcher swallowed and nodded. "We can go into the parlor."

"Yes, let's do," Mother said. Said the spider to the fly.

The parlor—on our right through sliding pocket doors—was all dark walls and somber Gothic furnishings, marginally cheered by the morning sun.

Mother and I sat on a couch with cushions somewhat softer than stone near a baroque carved fireplace while Mrs. Hatcher helped herself to a high-backed chair with pointed finials that looked lethal.

I couldn't seem to reconcile the surroundings with the mayor's country-club persona. Had this (to me) hideous mansion been inherited? Or perhaps it reflected his wife's tastes?

The woman began, "Myron worked at the store late last night, cleaning up."

Mother was still cross-examining the furnishings, so I said, "Why was that necessary?"

She sighed. "Because things were such a mess, what with everyone searching for that Poe prize. More like locusts than customers." She shrugged and shook her head. "Anyway, I wasn't too worried when he hadn't come home by the time I went to bed. It's been like this on previous fest weekends as well."

Mother had finally turned her attention to the mayor's wife. "When exactly did he usually get home, Mrs. Hatcher, during Poe Days?"

"Call me Caroline, please. About midnight. But I woke around three and Myron still wasn't here, so I called his cell phone. When he didn't answer, I tried the shop's number and got the answering machine." She paused. "Then at six this morning I called Paula Baxter—her store is next door, and she has an apartment above her place. She says she hasn't seen Myron since a meeting at city hall early last evening."

A tear trailed down the woman's cheek, and she wiped it away with a forefinger.

"Go on, Caroline," Mother said. "And I'm Vivian. And this is my deputy."

I didn't know whether to growl or laugh, and did neither.

Caroline said, "I asked Paula if she'd go down to our shop and see if Myron might have worked through the night—or fallen asleep there."

The deputy—me, remember?—asked, "Why didn't you go straight there yourself?"

"I didn't want to leave the house, in case Myron came home. Well, Paula called me back and said the front door was locked and he didn't answer her knock. And she knocked hard. So she went around to the back door—also locked—and saw that his *car* was still there! She pounded the back door and got no response, then called me. And that's when I got in touch with you, Deputy."

"Call me Brandy, please."

Mother gave me a mildly reproving glance, as if that were inappropriate, then asked Caroline if Myron had any enemies.

This question startled Mrs. Hatcher, who sat forward. "Why . . . why do you ask? Do you think something may have happened to him? That someone might have . . . done something?"

"No, no," Mother replied soothingly. "It's just a routine question, Caroline."

The woman's chin rose, her expression at least a little

indignant. "Well, he didn't have an enemy in the world! Everyone loves Myron."

"I'm sure they did," Mother said.

"Did?"

"Do. I'm sure they do." She was backpedaling like a circus monkey on a unicycle. "I'm sure Anitqua's well-regarded mayor will turn up perfectly well with a perfectly good explanation."

And that assurance proved perfectly useless, as Mrs. Hatcher's worried expression returned, buying none of it.

"Myron has *never* disappeared like this before," the woman said. "And after what happened to that poor girl yesterday—"

She began to cry.

I got up and gave our hostess a tissue from my purse, then returned to my post.

Mother leaned forward. "Try not to worry yourself, dear, we will find him. By the by . . . whose idea was it, living here?"

Caroline, thrown by this non sequitur, frowned above the tissue she was using and said, "What?"

"Ancestral home, is it?"

Mrs. Hatcher shook her head. "No. Myron always had his eye on this place, ever since we moved to Antiqua. When it came up for sale, we snatched it up. But it's been something of a money pit, and sometimes we kick ourselves for . . ." She frowned, angry either at herself or Mother for getting off-track (perhaps both). "You *will* find him, won't you, Sheriff?"

"Never have I, in holding this office, failed to locate a missing person."

That seemed to reassure Caroline Hatcher, at least a little, probably because she didn't realize that her husband was Mother's first missing person.

Before we took our leave, Mother asked for and received a key to the Hatchers' antiques shop and a spare key fob to Myron's Cadillac.

Back in the Explorer, the near-mansion looming over us like a solid shadow, I remarked, "I don't know why you like Gothic Revival."

"In this instance, I don't particularly. The Hatcher manse is rather beyond the pale, don't you think? Did you ever wonder what that expression means, dear?"

"Can't say that I have." Actually, I thought it was "beyond the pail," like maybe somebody threw a paintbrush at a can and missed.

"It refers to an area in Ireland," Mother said, with the characteristic smugness she assumed when schooling her backward daughter, "where the wealthy once lived—from Dundalk to south of Dublin."

I started the engine up. "Gee, now I can check that one off my 'ever wonder' list. Anything else you'd care to share?"

She put a finger to her lips. "Just a question. Did you notice the state of structural disrepair?"

"How can you tell with Gothic?"

"And the sparseness of the furniture in the parlor, along with missing pictures, as evidenced by their outlines on the faded wallpaper? I sense financial difficulties." In transit now, I offered a one-shouldered shrug. "They own two late-model cars. Besides, maybe some of the furniture and framed pictures have been moved to their store to sell this weekend."

Mother sighed. "I suppose that's *one* explanation."

"Or maybe the stuff didn't come with the place. My guess is, it's a dream house that turned out to be a nightmare. Way too big and demanding for a couple. So they'll eventually sell it."

Mother said nothing. She hated it when I shot down any of her notions.

"Anyway," I said, "we've got an M.I.A. mayor to find."

Antiqua was bustling once again, but entering from the south was easy, and I quickly found my way, via side streets, to the alley behind the row of antiques stores.

And, as Paula had told Mrs. Hatcher, the mayor's silver Cadillac was parked near the back door of Top Drawer.

I eased the Explorer over, leaving some distance between us and the Caddy, and we both climbed out.

Staying by the SUV, I watched as Mother moved slowly around the car, peering in the windows. After trying the door handles and finding them locked, she used the key remote to access the inside and root around, including the trunk.

I was getting hot standing in the sun, the cooler morning air having evaporated.

"Well?" I asked, impatiently.

She walked over. "Nothing seems untoward." Digging out the spare key to the shop, she said, "Let's have a look inside."

Nothing seemed "untoward" in there, either.

The high-end, somewhat pretentious (IMHO) antiques were nicely arranged and well displayed, with no signs of a robbery or a scuffle. The checkout counter was neat and tidy, as were the undisturbed contents of the drawers—everything ready for today's onslaught.

The only thing missing was the store's owner.

I heard the front door unlock, and we looked that way in anticipation; a male teenager in a short-sleeved white shirt and blue jeans entered, along with a warm breeze.

"Oh!" the young man said, startled at the sight of us. He was pudgy, with sand-colored hair and a cherubic face.

Mother, not bothering to explain what we were doing there and how we got in, asked, "And what is *your* name?"

"Ryan, sir . . . er, ma'am . . . I mean, Sheriff."

"Have you seen Mr. Hatcher recently?"

He took a few tentative steps forward. "Not since I closed up yesterday. Is . . . is something wrong?"

"No," Mother said. "Will you ask him to call Sheriff Borne when he comes in? He has my number."

"Okay."

We left through the back, Mother locking the door behind us.

Outside, I took a stroll around the Caddy myself, then knelt on the gravel to look under the car.

Mother, heels of her hands resting on her duty belt, in a vague suggestion of Western sheriff, said, "Dear, you're wasting your time."

I stood, and mimicked her hands-on-hips pose. "Am I?" Then I held out the mayor's key fob.

Mother beamed. "Well, what do you think about that!"

I took that literally and said, "He could have dropped it when somebody grabbed him. Could this be a kidnapping?"

"A snatch job?" she said. I hated it when she talked like somebody in an old *Hawaii Five-O* episode. "We don't know that for certain. There could be any number of reasons for that key fob getting under there."

"You do realize we should inform the FBI, don't you?"

She made a "What For?" face and shrugged.

I smirked. "You don't want to do that, because they would take over."

"I *will* call them," she said, with just a hint of defensiveness, "if and when we have more proof to back up your theory."

"More proof than the shop owner disappeared last night and his key fob was found under his Cadillac? And, by the way, we just had a murder in this small town?"

"I have no intention of wasting the FBI's time. They

have enough to do, trying to decide who in government to go after next."

I sighed. "I just don't want you to get yourself in trouble. You're only getting started in this job." Which reminded me. "What happened at the casino? You were following a lead, right?"

She nodded. "Morella Crafton went to the Tomahawk Thursday night, and their security team may be able to provide us with camera coverage of a cell call she received. Possibly including the caller's number."

"Anything else?"

"No."

Mother had a "tell" when she was lying: Her eyes looked briefly to the right. But, for now, I didn't press the point.

She was saying, "I need to use our mobile radio to check in with Deputy Chen, then contact the coroner for his prelim findings on Morella. With luck, the casino may have found that video by now. But for the moment our chief concern is the missing mayor."

"Right," I said. "How about tracking the mayor's cell phone?"

Mother nodded. "The PD might be able to assist with that—*if* his phone is still turned on. For now, I need to stay at the scene. But there's something you can do."

"What?"

"Interview the council members. Find out when they last had contact with His Honor. Then ask them to frankly discuss any adversaries he might have. Even a small-town mayor can make enemies."

"Roger that."

Mother held out a hand. "I'll need the keys to the SUV, dear, to engage the equipment—computer, mobile radio, and such."

"Use your own key," I said.

"Why, what key would that be?"

"Oh! Don't you have one tucked away in your utility belt, Batman? Or did you hot-wire the SUV last night?"

And I walked away.

She could always fire me.

I had not been inside the other council members' shops and was curious to see what the contents revealed about the owners' personalities, the way Top Drawer Antiques had the pretentious Myron Hatcher.

(I would hate to think what our merchandise back at Trash 'n' Treasures said about Mother and me, especially since it included a lacquered fruitcake, a Happy Face alarm clock, and a tabletop plastic Christmas tree for weenies on toothpicks.)

Paula Baxter's redundantly named Relics Antiques was open for business, although not very busy despite the festival. Which actually made sense, as people were waiting for the release of the second encrypted clue at noon to further indicate exactly what Poe item they would be looking for.

Paula—in an orange-red dress that went well with her short red hair—was behind the counter, waiting on a customer, giving me the opportunity to stroll around her shop.

The place had a casual vibe, the antiques fairly common and only slightly overpriced. Unlike Top Drawer, where placards screamed "Prices Firm," I had the feeling you might be able to bargain with Paula.

Many antiques shop owners bought what they themselves liked and even collected, since they had to be around the stuff all day—and items suitable for their own collections might be brought to them by dealers and clients. Paula offered a diverse assortment of furniture, glassware, old toys, and books, with a penchant for vintage Christmas items, as well as a fondness for framed pictures (some oil, some prints) of old-time, homey settings—snow-covered farmhouses, cozy cottages at autumn, families gathered 'round the hearth, and so on.

Paula was free now, so I walked over to the counter.

Immediately she asked, "Any word from Myron?"

"No. But we did speak at some length to Caroline. She seems pretty flummoxed, has no idea what might have happened."

She shook her head. "I just don't understand it. Myron is supposed to hand out the second clue soon!"

If he'd been kidnapped, that would seem the least of our concerns; but right now in Antiqua, the festival was all.

I shrugged, not sure what to say. "Well, it's not noon yet."

Her eyes brightened. "I'm *sure* he'll show up by then. He loves the limelight too much to miss it."

"When did you last see Myron?"

"Yesterday," she said without pause, "after our stores closed. We had a quick meeting at city hall about how we felt things were going with the fest. That lasted, oh, maybe . . . fifteen minutes?"

"Any idea where Myron might have gone after that?"

"Sure. Back to his shop. We walked over together. My place looked like a tornado blew through it."

"You stayed to clean up the place?"

"Yes."

"For how long?"

She made a face, shrugged. "Finally gave up around nine. Went upstairs—that's where I live. I mean, what's the point of spending *too much* time putting everything back in perfect place? Folks are going to mess things up even more today."

I nodded. "Did the mayor have any enemies you know of? Political opponents, maybe?"

Her eyes narrowed. "Do you mean someone who might want to do him harm? Physical harm?"

I nodded again.

She shook her head, kind of shivered. "Then, no, I can't think of anyone."

Paula's eyes shifted from mine to someone who had just come in, and for a brief moment her eyes registered surprise. And what else?

Alarm?

I turned to see a man on the near side of middle-age, about six foot, maybe one hundred eighty pounds, wearing a wrinkled plaid shirt, baggy blue jeans, and scuffed white tennis shoes. His long, graying hair pulled back in a ponytail and the unruly salt-and-pepper beard gave me the impression of an aging hippie.

"Welcome to Relics Antiques," Paula said cordially. No sign of alarm now. "Let me know if I can be of any help."

He approached. "I'm looking for a turn-of-the-century candlestick telephone."

Paula smiled. "I believe I have one."

She threw the smile at me. "You'll have to excuse me, Ms. Borne."

"That was all, anyway," I told her. "Let the sheriff know if you hear from Myron. Right away."

"Will do."

She disappeared with the man into the back of the store. I went outside, where the sidewalk was beginning to bustle with jovial, mildly crazed folks, ready to continue the search.

I'd become pretty adept at quickly scanning and mentally recording merchandise in other antiques shops, always on the lookout for something unique for us. I'd have remembered seeing a vintage candlestick phone in Paula's store, as it would have made a perfect addition to ours, specifically the living room Victorian merchandise. But I supposed I could have missed it.

Lottie Everhart's shop Somewhere in Time—judging by Mother's earlier description of the place as having been filled to the rafters and cluttered—seemed to have changed dramatically since the death of the proprietress's partner.

The store was more of a gift shop now, with antiques scattered here and there as almost an afterthought. It was as if Lottie had wanted to expunge any memory of the store prior to the disastrous Poe portrait sale and the suicide of her husband, Mike.

I located the owner, attractive in a low-cut white blouse and tight black slacks (her, not me), as she was opening a glass display case of Precious Moments figurines for a heavyset woman whose face at rest seemed to form a permanent frown.

Lottie handed a small collectible—a baby with a bear on its back—to the customer, who skeptically looked at the price, then sniffed, "I can get it cheaper on the Internet."

The customer thrust the figurine back at Lottie and trundled off.

Looking at me, the owner sighed. "You don't know how many times I hear that."

Me too. My answer to such a patron in our store? "By all means, spend less money if you can. On the other hand, the item you desire is right here, right now . . . and you can examine it, and take it home to enjoy, immediately. Without fear of having it mischaracterized on the Internet or arriving damaged in the mail."

Worked for me, almost always.

But sharing this perhaps unwanted advice was not why I was here. It was to say, "I need to speak with you."

"Certainly," Lottie replied. "Won't get crazy in here until noon." She replaced the little figurine on a shelf, locked the case, then turned to me.

I informed the council member that the mayor hadn't been seen since their meeting yesterday evening.

Lottie frowned and said, "Well, that's odd. He seemed perfectly fine then. And Caroline has no idea where he is?"

"No. Can you think of anyone who might wish him harm?"

Her eyes widened. "Good heavens, no! Certainly not! He's something of a beloved figure around town."

That seemed to be the consensus.

I pressed. "Mr. Hatcher ever have a run-in with anyone? Any bad blood from a political opponent when he ran for office, for instance?"

"Well . . ."

I waited.

She moved a step closer and lowered her voice, though the shop was otherwise empty. "A few weeks ago, after our regular meeting at city hall? Myron and Wally stayed behind in the conference room. I was about to go out the front door when I heard them."

"Heard them what?"

She hesitated, then said, "Arguing."

"About . . . ?"

She shook her head. "No idea. The conference door was closed. But voices *were* raised."

I said, "The sheriff will want to know more about that."

Lottie shrugged. "Nothing more to share, really. Disagreements come up among us all the time. We don't always see eye to eye—that doesn't make us enemies." She touched my arm. "If Myron *is* missing, what does it mean?"

"I honestly don't know," was my reply.

And with Mother still keeping the lid on Morella's death being a murder, I dare not add that to the mix.

I left a concerned Lottie behind and went two doors down to Wally's Junk 'n' Stuff, where upon entering I began to sneeze.

No dusting seemed to have been done in here for years. Stuff was stacked everywhere—paint-peeling doors, seatless chairs, rusty metal, moldy books, cracked crockery. A neon TILT sign flashed in my brain as I tried to take it all in.

Narrow aisles—sometimes leading to dead ends—had visitors jostling around one another. This mess, after all, would seem an ideal place to hide something. I found the owner wearing the same short-sleeved plaid shirt and well-worn cargo shorts as the day before, singing the praises of an old wooden wagon wheel to a male customer, who decided to take a pass when his wife elbowed him helpfully.

After informing Wally I needed a word, he said he was too busy for that, so I let him know the sheriff had sent me. He sighed—I was surprised a blast of dust didn't come out—and we snaked our way back to a dirty and dusty office, where we stood facing each other.

After I filled him in, Wally echoed what Paula and Lottie had said about seeing Myron at the meeting last night. He said he was sure the mayor would turn up.

"You had an argument with him a while back," I reminded him, "after another recent meeting."

"Says who?"

"Not at liberty to say."

"Lottie!" he scoffed. "She's a little snoop and a trouble-maker who oughtta look after her own affairs, if you get my drift."

This was not the quiet, emotional man I had met at the church (and Mother had not yet shared with me her encounter with him at Morella's apartment upstairs).

I asked, "What was the argument with Mayor Hatcher about?"

"Didn't Lottie tell you? I mean, she probably had her *ear* to the door!"

I said nothing.

He sighed. "I was just . . . ticked off that Myron took over the planning of this year's festival, wholesale, including picking the prize—which we *all* had to chip in for, so why didn't we have more of a say in it?"

The question was rhetorical, so I waited.

"Anyway," Wally went on, "that's water under the bridge."

"Then you're happy with the choice of the Poe book?"

He shrugged a single shoulder. "I guess it was worth the price. Attendance is up at the festival, which should mean more sales. And Myron promised to make picking any future prizes a joint effort. *After* the fact, but he did promise."

Regarding any enemies Mr. Hatcher might have, the junk dealer couldn't think of any, somewhat reluctantly admitting that Myron was generally well liked, even if Wally and Myron had their share of disagreements.

Before departing, I asked Wally what he was going to do with Morella's things—mostly to gauge his reaction—and his demeanor immediately softened.

"I don't really know," he said sadly. "She didn't have any relatives. I guess when the sheriff says it's okay, I'll box up what's there and donate it someplace."

"Sounds right," I said, then smiled a little and left.

My final stop took up much of the next block—Rick's Treasure Aisles, an old barn reconverted into an antiques mall with dozens of booths rented by different dealers. Such malls were my favorite antiques shopping experience—you never knew what you might find. Each stall was different: This one sloppy, that one neat, next one focused, its neighbor scattered. And the barn atmosphere itself was charming and relaxed.

I found Rick trying to deal with two customers, with another waiting for his attention. I took the owner's arm and pulled him aside.

Our brief conversation wasn't worth the paper we've printed it on. But you better read it, anyway.

Me: Excuse me, but no one can find Mr. Hatcher.

Rick: So what?

Me: I mean he's missing.

Rick: Who cares?

Me: Did anyone hate him?

Rick: Everybody hated him. If they say different, they're lying. Now, if you're not gonna buy something? I'm busy.

Walking back to rejoin Mother, I passed city hall, where Paula was passing out slips of paper with the second cryptogram. She saw me through the crowd, raised her eyebrows in question, as if to ask, "Any news about Myron?" I shook my head in answer. Our shared expression said the mayor must be in trouble.

I picked up an undeciphered sheet someone had dropped on the ground.

0++! 1+(.+8@) 2++! 8*;6;08= ;508)

From my purse I got out a pen and the cheat sheet of codes I'd recorded so far and began marking up the new cryptogram, right there on the sidewalk.

This clue was harder, but since I already knew what the prize was, it didn't take me long, even with a few gaps of letters, like on *Wheel of Fortune*:

Look for Poe's book entitled Tales.

My cell phone rang.

"Come at once," Mother said urgently. "I'm still in the alley behind Top Drawer."

"On my way."

I broke into a jog, and by the time I reached the Explorer—within which Mother was seated behind the wheel, tempting fate, with the air conditioner running—my clothes were soaked.

I got in on the rider's side. "What is it?" I asked, out of breath.

"Myron's cell phone has been triangulated to the church," she said, eyes bright with the excitement of the chase.

Mine widened too; no idea whether they were bright (kind of doubt it). "Not *another* entombment?"

"*Inside* the church," she clarified.

I got out, Mother got out, and we performed what in less enlightened days might be termed a Chinese fire drill. Soon I was behind the wheel, and we got going.

On the short drive to the church, Mother told me that the coroner had reported having a hard time estimating the time of Morella's death—due to the heat—but felt the young woman had likely died between midnight and two a.m. Since she had been alive in the sarcophagus for a while, Morella could have been attacked much earlier.

But it wouldn't have taken her too long to run out of air.

I asked, "And word from the casino?"

"Nothing yet."

The front doors of the church was unlocked per usual, and we entered, the sheriff leading, deputy following. That much in our relationship hadn't changed.

Pastor Creed, placing hymnals in the wooden holders on the back of pews, paused in his toil as we approached.

"Good morning—or should I say afternoon," he said pleasantly. "Another hot one." Then, reading our expressions, he added, "Is anything wrong?"

Mother didn't bother answering; instead she got out her cell phone and quickly entered a number.

Pastor Creed asked, "What is this about?"

"Triangulation indicates," I said, "that Mayor Hatcher's cell phone is *here* somewhere."

"It is?" The pastor frowned in confusion. "What are you—"

The trill of a cell phone rose faintly through the floorboards.

Mother demanded of the confused pastor, "Take me to the basement. Now."

"The only entry," he said, pointing, "is outside in back."

Mother moved faster than anyone who'd recently had bunion surgery should have been able. I followed her, and the man of God followed me.

As Mother neared the slanted wooden doors leading to the basement, the pastor called out, "Sheriff! You're not going *down* there are you?"

She put on the brakes. "Why? Don't you *want* me to?"

Creed, out of breath, said, "You just need to take care if you do! The workmen likely left a mess when they quit yesterday, and they're not due back till Monday."

Mother looked past the pastor. "Brandy, your assistance please."

She and I grabbed the handles on the storm cellar doors, and in seconds we were descending a half flight of wooden steps, Creed trailing behind. The trilling had stopped, gone to voice mail probably.

The basement—really a large, low-ceilinged cellar—had a dirt floor and red brick walls. Scattered about, as the pastor promised, were the workmen's hand tools, several wheelbarrows, bags of mortar, and stacks of bricks.

Behind us, the pastor—still not getting it—said, "There's nothing to see down here. Just some crumbling walls that need replacing." Then: "*That's* odd. . . ."

Creed walked over to a recently constructed wall, touched it, and said, "This shouldn't be out so far."

Mother's grin was a skull's. "'The Cask of Amontillado'!"

Again she entered the mayor's number . . .

. . . *and the trill came from behind the wall!*

"Brandy! Get a tool—you too, Pastor. *Anything* we can use to break through this brick. Let's hope it hasn't dried too thoroughly."

"Wait!" Creed protested. "What . . . ?"

"Do as she says," I told him.

I grabbed a flat-edged shovel, Mother took a mortar hoe, and the pastor reluctantly found a heavy stone-hammer.

Together we pounded on the bricks, which easily broke apart because the mortar had, thankfully, not set.

And there, on his knees on the dirt floor in the tight space, his wrists clasped to the crumbling wall behind him, was the slumped, head-hanging figure of a man, a rag stuffed in his mouth as a gag.

Someone had entombed the mayor.

A Trash 'n' Treasures Tip

The old adage that good things come to those who wait can apply to hunting for rare books. Be patient, and it will turn up. Patience, though, is not one of Mother's virtues, or mine . . . and certainly not Sushi's, who is still with us despite having chewed up one of Mother's favorite tomes, *Rebecca of Sunnybrook Farm* (not *Rebecca of Manderley*).

Chapter Six

Poe With the Flow

My first impression was that the mayor was dead, but then a soft, muffled moan emerged from the cloth stuffed in his mouth. He moved a little.

"He's alive!" I said, and immediately realized I sounded like Colin Clive in the 1931 *Frankenstein*.

The pastor and I stepped aside to give Mother room as she crouched before the hole we had made in the brick wall. Reaching in, she touched Mr. Hatcher's arm, and he emitted a louder groan.

She leaned in and snatched the cloth from his lips. "Myron!" she said. "Wakey wakey!"

"Huh? . . . What . . . ?" came the weak reply.

"We're going to widen the hole," Mother told the prisoner. "Don't go anywhere."

The mayor's head came up, and he goggled at her. Apparently he would honor her request.

We used the tools and widened the aperture. Mother had me take photos of the crime scene before the pastor used a screwdriver to pry loose the clasps that had been hammered into the wall—wasn't terribly hard removing them, since that wall was rather a crumbling thing in the first place.

Mother took the half-sitting man by one arm and said, "Pastor Creed, some assistance please."

Mother's low-back issues wouldn't allow her to perform this duty alone. Creed took the mayor's other arm—Myron's suit was powdered with pulverized mortar from his rescue—and they helped him through the hole. I continued to take pictures on my phone of the procedure.

"Where . . . where the hell am I?" the mayor asked groggily, leaning heavily on the pastor.

Who said, "*Language*, please."

"The church basement," Mother told him.

Myron's words came slowly. "My . . . head . . . hurts. Really *hurts*. What . . . happened?"

Mother said, "You may have been sapped, Mayor Hatcher."

"Sapped?"

"That's what we call 'conked' in the law enforcement game. Do you think you can walk?"

He nodded, then said, "Need water. And . . . a restroom. Any . . . any of you see my glasses?"

"We'll tend to your needs," Mother replied, then nodded to me to go in through that hole and have a look around and snap some more pics. She and the pastor drunk-walked the mayor toward the stone steps to the outdoors.

Checking inside the would-be tomb, I saw nothing in the dirt but chunks and shards of broken mortar and brick—no sign of His Honor's glasses. Outside the opening, any footprints the abductor might have left had been obliterated by our own movements—that and the action of dragging Mr. Hatcher out of captivity.

Expanding my search, I found several cigarette butts, along with a crumpled Camels pack, which I believed to have been left by a workman. I doubted that the killer would have built the wall, then hung around for a few smokes. Discovery of another empty Camels pack, and more spent butts, seemed to substantiate that theory.

Above, a toilet flushed and water pipes gurgled; I left the basement, closing the storm cellar doors, and headed inside to join the others in the sanctuary.

They were down in front, Mayor Hatcher (in the first pew) the only one seated. Mother was in the row behind the mayor, leaning over to press a white hand towel to the back of his head. Pastor Creed stood before his lone parishioner, holding a glass of water.

Mother was saying, "There isn't any blood . . . just a nasty little bump. But you really should go to the ER."

"No, I'm all right," the mayor responded, sounding more like himself.

"You were apparently unconscious for nearly twelve hours, Mr. Hatcher," Mother told him. "A possible concussion is nothing to play fast and loose with."

Hatcher held up a hand and glanced back at her, signaling that she should cease the toweling. "I said I'm fine. I appreciate your concern, Sheriff . . . Pastor. But what *happened* to me?"

"That's what I hope to find out from *you*," Mother replied, moving into the aisle to see him better.

He frowned up at her. "I'll do what I can, only . . . I can't remember a thing."

"You must try. Because I can tell you one very obvious thing: Someone tried to kill you, and in a most nasty way."

Hatcher swallowed thickly, then thrust his hand toward Pastor Creed, gesturing for the glass of water, which his holy host provided. After the mayor downed its contents, he handed the glass back with a nod of thanks.

Then, staring past the preacher at the large, looming cross on the wall, the mayor said, "All I remember is leaving the back of the store around midnight, walking to my car, and . . . really, that's . . . that's all." His eyes went to Mother. "The next thing I'm aware of is being in a cold, musty place, in a kind of sitting position on a hard surface . . . and you talking to me."

Not much to go on.

Mother nodded for the mayor to make room, and he did, sliding over. She sat next to Myron, angled toward him.

"Would you do something for me?" she asked. "It might be unpleasant, but it could be most helpful."

"I'll . . . I'll certainly try."

"Good. Close your eyes."

"Close my . . . ?

"Close your eyes. That's right. Now go back to the moment you were leaving the store. You've been working late, you are tired, you want to get home to Caroline. You have your keys to the store in your hand and lock the back door."

"No need. It locks when I shut it . . . but I do have my car key fob in hand."

"Fine. You go down the few stairs to the alley. What then?"

"I click the car open, with the fob."

"Excellent," Mother said. "The car lights are now on and you walk toward the driver's side, the key fob in your hand. You reach for the door handle."

Hatcher's eyes flew open. "I see a figure behind me! Reflected in the window glass!"

"Who?" Mother asked, excitedly.

The mayor shook his head, but it seemed to hurt and he stopped. "Indistinct . . . little more than a shadow."

Mother looked deflated. "Little more?"

The mayor hesitated. "And yet . . ."

"Yes? Yes? Yes?" One more "yes" and maybe I *would* kick her in the sanctuary.

The mayor was saying, "I *did* form . . . an impression of someone."

"A specific someone?"

"Yes."

"Someone with a *name?*"

"Yes."

"Well?"

He seemed strangely embarrassed. "Edgar Allan Poe. Have I lost my senses?"

Mother sighed. "Not necessarily. After all, he's very much on everyone's mind."

Pastor Creed offered, "Maybe it was someone in a Poe costume . . . like yours, Sheriff."

"Perhaps," Mother conceded, glancing at me.

We were having the same thought, I felt sure. Was some off-the-wall killer dressing up like the festival's honored subject and re-creating the long-dead author's fictional homicides?

The mayor, blinking, getting his bearings finally, said, "I should call my wife. I really should. Caroline must be terribly worried."

This had occurred to me the moment we'd found him, but I knew Mother would want to question the man (no matter his condition) before his wife arrived in hysterics to spirit him understandably away.

And, perhaps five minutes later—in response to the call her husband made on the phone that had led to his rescue—his wife burst into the church and flew down the aisle to wrap her arms around her husband, who had risen to meet her, Mother scooting out of their way.

When Mrs. Hatcher finally unwound herself, her damp eyes went to Mother, then Creed, then me, and back to Mother. "Who would *do* such a thing?" Her husband had filled her in on the phone. "Everyone in Antiqua *loves* Myron!"

"Apparently not everyone," Mother said.

"I don't understand," Caroline said crossly. "First Morella is found dead, now someone tries to *kill* my husband—and nearly succeeded!"

Creed was nodding. "And might well have if Sheriff Borne hadn't thought to try calling his cell phone here in the church."

Mother explained how triangulation had led us here.

She went on, "I have come to the conclusion that someone is trying—in the most despicable and diabolical fashion—to disrupt this festival. But for what purpose I cannot say." She paused. "Therefore I must insist that it be shut down, toot sweet."

"I agree," Pastor Creed said.

I felt the same, but a part of me was wondering if Mother would be making this suggestion if she hadn't already given her performance of "The Raven."

"*No!*" the mayor protested, eyes popping as if he were Peter Lorre. "Then the fiend who's *doing* these evil things will *win!*"

Mother shook her head somberly and placed a gentle hand on the mayor's shoulder. "I can't risk another attempt on some other victim's life."

Myron gave her a narrow-eyed, rather shrewd look. "But you *can* risk not *catching* this person? Is that really your best option? And if we cancel the festival, the murderer will leave Antiqua, along with everyone else. He . . . or she . . . will be in the wind."

Mother was frowning thoughtfully. "You're assuming the 'he or she' is a stranger, not someone in town?"

"Sheriff, I know everyone in Antiqua. I suppose it's possible that a local is responsible. But based upon the nature of these crimes, doesn't it appear that a psychopath has been drawn here, responding in some sick way to the dark

ANTIQUES RAVIN' 103

side of Poe's work? If you close down this event, it seems likely the murderer will be beyond your grasp."

Mother looked at me. I was oddly complimented that she wanted my opinion.

I gave it to her with a shrug. "The mayor's point is valid. Maybe Morella's necklace and Mr. Hatcher's car key fob were meant to be found, to announce a Poe-style crime. Not closing down the fest might be worth the risk."

I had a reason for going out on this precarious limb, which I intended to act upon very soon.

Caroline was saying, "I don't give a damn about this stupid festival—I'm taking Myron to the hospital right now!"

Hatcher took his wife firmly yet lovingly by her shoulders, saying in earnest, "Please do this my way, dear, and I *promise* you I'll go for a complete checkup on Monday."

She was near tears. "You could have some bad effects from the blow in the meantime. . . ."

"If so, we'll go straight to the hospital. Immediately."

She was weakening. "Well . . . in that case . . . whatever you and the sheriff decide, I'll support."

The mayor addressed Mother. "Sheriff, what if I go home, clean up, then come back for the announcement of the final cryptogram at four o'clock? Wouldn't you imagine the killer might be shocked to see me, alive and well, and react in some way?"

Mother was nodding slowly. It was an idea so crazy she might have come up with it herself. She said, "Could be we'd flush him out."

"Or her," I said.

Caroline's eyes were wide and her tone was bitter. "So now Myron will be used as *bait?* Do you have any other bright ideas, Sheriff Borne?"

Mother replied reassuringly, "I'll be right at His Honor's side, my dear. As will the other council members, and you as well, if you wish."

"I still don't like it," Caroline said, if not quite as force-fully. "I don't like it at all."

As the discussion continued, I slipped outside to use my cell.

"Tony," I asked Serenity's chief of police, "are you still coming tonight?"

"Around seven. Why? That all right?"

"Could you make it earlier? I'm afraid Mother's in over her head. There are problems here."

"Well, maybe she needs to get a taste of what she's in for. She's going to have to either be up to the job or step down."

That sounds crueler than it was delivered. Tony was thinking of what was best for both Borne girls.

So I said, "What if I said *I* was in over *my* head too?"

"Tell me," he said.

I filled him in on the killer's latest Poe tribute.

"What time," he asked, "do you want me there?"

After Caroline Hatcher had piled her husband into their burgundy Buick and headed home, Mother once again called in the Serenity PD forensics, to go over the mayor's car and the area around it, and the church basement, warning them that the latter location had been trampled and otherwise disturbed in the rescue of the attempted murder victim.

Mother did not inform the FBI about Myron's abduc-tion, deeming it unnecessary now that the mayor had been found. This seemed perfectly reasonable to me, for a change, but proved a decision (among others) for which she would later pay a price; for now, Sheriff Vivian Borne acted as she saw fit, with her sort-of-deputy's blessing.

While Mother hung around at the church, waiting for forensics, I went back to the Pullman to see what revenge a neglected Sushi might have wrought upon her mistress.

That she did not greet me at the door was not a good
sign. I found her curled up on the couch, refusing to ac-
knowledge me with even a glance. So of course I explained
why I had been away for so long, apologizing profusely, as
if she could understand (and suspecting that she could).

I had been living out of my suitcase, which was open on
the floor next to the couch; on top of my clothes was a
perfect little cigar-shaped prezzie to let me know just how
unhappy she was.

But I knew of a way to get back in her good graces.

I dispensed with the cigar, went over and picked up the little rascal, then headed with her back out into the sultry heat.
A few minutes later, we were entering the air-conditioned
bakery, its proprietor behind the glass counter wearing his
usual confectionary-stained white apron.

"Hi, George," I said, as we were now on a first-name
basis.

"Hello, Brandy . . . Sushi," he said with a smile. "Another scorcher, huh?"

"Not hot enough to keep us away from some more
doggie cookies."

"How many?"

I gauged what would get me out of the doghouse. "Four
please." Studying what remained of his stock, I added,
"And a bear claw for me."

Sushi gave my cheek a little lick, signaling her snit was
over.

"But," I told her firmly, "you're not getting any of mine."

This she seemed not to understand. Which means she did.

George prepared two small, white sacks and set them by
the cash register. He was about to calculate the price, when
he paused to ask, "Any progress on finding Morella's killer?"

This startled me. I'd hoped the supposition that the
young woman's passing was due to an overdose would

have held sway a little longer. But, then, this was a small town.

Not bothering to deny it, I said, "Sorry, if I knew any-thing—which I don't—I really couldn't tell you."

Not snippily or anything.

"Yes, of course," he said with a nod. "It's just that, well . . . I did notice something on the afternoon of the day she disappeared. It might not *mean* anything."

"You noticed something?" I prompted.

He nodded again. "I'd been taking a smoke break in the alley and was about to go back inside. That's when I saw Morella coming out the back of the coffee shop and walk-ing over to your mother's car . . . the sheriff's SUV? I could see it parked in front of city hall. Anyway, she stuck some-thing under the wiper. Like maybe a note or a notice about an event or something. Then she went back in to work. Did you get it?"

"Get it?"

"Whatever she put on the windshield."

"Oh, yeah. It was an Edgar Allan Poe quote."

"Oh," George said disappointedly.

"Appreciate the info, though. How much do I owe you?"

When he handed me back my change, both the bills and the change included doggie cookie crumbs.

Walking toward the coffee shop, hands laden with Sushi and sacks, I pondered Morella's motive behind the myste-rious quote: *"Believe nothing you hear and only half of what you see."*

Was it a warning?

If so, about what or who? Or had the note been intended to trigger an investigation, should something happen to her? Then, if nothing *did* happen, the missive would be for-gotten, shrugged off as more Poe nonsense in the midst of the festival.

One thing seemed certain, though, or anyway probable.

Morella Crafton had been involved in something she shouldn't have been.

Midafternoon, the coffee shop was hopping, visitors and locals alike sipping cool drinks in air-conditioned comfort while waiting for the release of the final crypto-clue.

I spotted Amy and Jessica—those two gossips from yesterday—sitting across from each other at a table for four. So I went over and asked if Sushi and I might join them. As I'd expected—since gossips are always eager for new news sources—I received an eager, positive response.

I settled in with Sushi on my lap, Amy on my left, Jessica on my right.

The two women were sharing another cheesecake. Both had bottled water, as if the noncalories of the latter would offset the off-the-charts calories of the former.

Willow wandered over and took my order of an iced tea, no sugar. (Yes, yes, I know—the noncalories of the sugarless iced tea would not offset my bear claw, either.)

Amy, the younger of the nosy pair, her long blond hair in a low-hanging ponytail today, said pleasantly, "So you're the sheriff's daughter!"

"That's right. I'm her pro bono deputy . . . which means I have zero authority to go along with the lack of pay."

They laughed politely at that. Meanwhile, single-minded Sushi barked for a cookie, and I dug into her sack.

Amy continued, overly friendly. "My, that must be interesting! What's it like?"

"Unpredictable. Mother can be what polite people might call eccentric. What people who *aren't* polite call her is . . . not polite."

Jessica, her brunette hair also pulled back, asked, "So, your main duty is driving her around?"

"I don't always chauffeur her." No need to go into Mother's driving history. Maybe they knew she'd driven to the casino and I'd be ratting her out if I mentioned her re-voked driver's license status. This pair seemed as if they knew about most everything in Antiqua.

Willow brought my tea, and I got out the bear claw.

Amy, dropping any chummy pretext, asked, "Why are the details of the Crafton girl's death being kept from the public?"

I took a big bite of the pastry, chewed, swallowed. "Because of further forensic evaluations."

Jessica leaned forward. "But she *was* murdered? That's what local gossips are saying."

She would know. Her and Amy.

"Yes," I said, making them work for it. Anyway, the bear claw was delicious.

Amy asked, "Does your mother know who is responsible?"

"Not yet." I wiped my mouth with a napkin. "But you nice gals might be able to assist."

Gossips love to help, especially when it provides rumors an extended life.

I asked, "What do you know about the mayor?"

"Well," Amy said, her eyes going big momentarily, "I know . . . or anyway, I *heard* . . . he didn't show up for dispensing the second clue today."

"What else?" I asked.

Jessica shrugged. "He likes to gamble."

I frowned. "Would you call him a gambling addict?"

"Not really," the older woman said. "But he's in over his head in debt, they say."

"From the gambling?"

Amy put in, "More from that run-down mansion of theirs, I'd wager."

"Why'd the Hatchers buy it," I asked, "if they couldn't afford the upkeep?"

The younger woman made a facial shrug. "Probably for appearance's sake. It used to belong to a wealthy landowner around here. And I think the mayor fancies himself in that class."

I took a sip of the cold tea. "What about the Hatcher's next-door shop neighbor, Paula Baxter?"

Jessica took the ball. "*She's* a strange one. Not unfriendly, but, well . . . aloof?"

Was she asking *me?* These uptalkers!

She was saying, "I tried to find out about her when she ran for city council . . . but she's not on social media. Only showed up on the Antiqua web page."

"An attractive woman," I said. "Is she dating anyone?"

Amy's shrug seemed oddly judgmental. "I never saw her with anyone of *either* sex."

Sushi barked for another cookie, and I wasn't about to argue. I didn't have enough clothes with me to risk another cigar-shaped present in my suitcase.

I asked, "What about Rick? He's kind of a hunk. What's his story?"

"Amy has a crush on him," Jessica said with a little laugh.

"But he's broke," Amy added, wrinkling her nose, indicating Rick was not worthy hookup material.

"Local boy?" I asked.

"That's right," Jessica said. "He inherited the antiques mall from his father, who wasn't much of a businessman either."

"Who has Rick dated?"

Amy lowered her voice. "There's been some talk about him and Lottie."

"*And* Mike," Jessica added, openly catty.

Even though I'd overheard this from them before, I didn't mind covering it again.

I asked, "You mean the shop owner who killed himself? After he sold the valuable Poe portrait?"

The older woman nodded. "But me? Personally?" She leaned forward and whispered, not really all that softly, "I'm not so sure it *was* suicide."

Amy took umbrage with her friend. "You shouldn't say such things, Jess. The authorities called it that."

The two were looking at each other now.

"Amy, you have to admit it was *strange*."

"Well, strange is one thing. Calling it something other than suicide is . . . well, that's strange too."

I asked, "Didn't he shoot himself? That's terribly sad, but nothing *strange* about it, really. Right?"

"He shot himself, yes," Jessica said, nodding. "In his garden, beneath a tree. But the strange part was what was hanging from a limb above him."

"What was that?"

"That," she said, "was the family cat."

The name of Poe's famous black cat leapt into my mind, claws out. "Pluto?" I asked breathlessly.

She reared back and looked at me funny. "No. Bing Clawsby."

"Was Bing Clawsby a *black* cat?"

The frown deepened. "Yellow."

Huh.

If Mr. Everhart's death had been an earlier Poe-style murder, the killer certainly did take some liberties with "The Black Cat."

Jessica was saying, in a somewhat hushed manner, "Anyway, if I had a devious mind, I might think *Lottie* killed Mike."

Amy, sotto voce, said, "Or Rick. Either Rick or Lottie, or the two of them together, if they'd been having their own affair."

"Lottie," I said, my mind spinning somewhat, "doesn't seem like the type who could kill a cat." Much less a person.

Jessica snorted. "Don't let Lottie fool you. She can be *vicious*. I've seen that firsthand at the nail shop."

But she didn't elaborate.

"Speaking of affairs," I said, "what about Wally Thorp and Morella? Could they have been having one? I mean, they would've made an odd couple, all right, but . . ."

The women's eyes met.

Then Jessica said to her friend, "Go ahead. It's the right thing to do."

Amy shifted in her chair. "I don't know exactly what was going on between them. I think Wally was definitely infatuated with her . . . but the feeling *clearly* wasn't reciprocated."

I asked, "Can you explain that?"

Amy nodded slowly. "Well, the infatuation part is based on him going out of his way not only to give the girl a place to live but financial support, too. I saw him slip her a wad of cash one day in the coffee shop!" She paused. "The not reciprocated part is because of the way she treated Wally—which is to say, like *dirt*. But she took his money, all right."

Jessica said, "And once I saw them arguing, out back of the coffee shop."

I asked, "About . . . ?"

She shook her head. "I was too far away to hear what it was about."

A first-rate gossip, like Mother, would have been able to lip-read.

Someone shouted, *"The third clue is out!"*

Suddenly folks bolted from their tables and began rushing out of the coffee shop. It was like a saloon in the Old West where everyone had just heard about a gold strike.

"Oh!" Amy exclaimed. "We've got to go!"

"Wish us luck," Jessica said, on her feet now. They pushed their chairs back in place, and Amy tossed a ten-dollar bill on the table.

Then they vaporized.

I left money for the tea and tip and wandered out onto the sidewalk with Sushi. A slip of paper fluttered by my feet. I stomped on it to a stop, and picked it up.

;48 2++! 6) 5; ;+. =(5]8(

Which I knew said that the Poe book was at Top Drawer, not because I'd memorized the code but because a mob was descending on the mayor's antiques store up the street.

Now, it seemed, might be a good time to drop in on Mr. Wally Thorp.

The narrow aisles of Junk 'n' Stuff were deserted, so I easily wound my way through the mounds of junk to the owner's untidy little office.

He was behind a metal desk, in a different short-sleeved plaid shirt (note that I did not say "fresh" short-sleeved plaid shirt), sitting there looking dejected, perhaps because his store was now empty of customers.

I knocked on the doorjamb to get his attention, and he looked my way, his head moving slowly on his neck.

I asked, "Can we talk?"

He shrugged. "I seem to have the time."

I approached the desk, then came right out with it. "Mr. Thorp, were you having an affair with Morella Crafton?"

His fleshy cheeks reddened. "No. Of course not."

"But weren't you giving her money on a regular basis?"

He stood, the chair rolling backward and then hitting the wall with a clunk. "Who told you *that?*"

"Someone who saw you giving her a handful of cash." I added, "And the sheriff knows from Morella's bank statements that the young woman was depositing *more* than her paycheck."

His sigh took a while. "All right . . . yes. I was helping her out. Two hundred bucks a week—what crime is there in that?"

"None, but what reason is there for it? You were also seen having an argument with her. What about?"

He almost snarled his answer. "I don't have to tell you a damn thing."

Sushi, in my arms, not liking his tone, growled.

"Better to tell me now," I said, "than the sheriff in an interview room at the Serenity county jail."

Wally thought about that. "I just . . . well, I didn't think she was making . . . good decisions for herself."

"What made it your business?"

He shrugged. "Just trying to help out a decent kid. I don't care what it looked like, that's what she was . . . a nice kid. Just a little . . . confused."

"In what way?"

"I . . . I thought she was dating someone she shouldn't."

"A married man possibly?"

He swallowed. "She denied it, but the way she was sneaking around? That's how I took it. I didn't believe her when she said otherwise."

"You were jealous," I said.

"No!"

Another growl from Sushi.

"You were in love with her," I pressed, leaning toward him, "and she rebuffed you."

"It wasn't like that at all. Not at all!"

"I see," I said with some sarcasm. "It was more like a *fatherly* thing."

Wally dropped down into the chair, and his shoulders slumped.

"Yes, it was," he said. "You see . . . I *am* her father."

And he fell back into his chair, burying his head in his hands, elbows on the armrests.

Stunned, I said, "I'm . . . I'm *sorry*, Mr. Thorp. I had no idea."

His eyes, filled with tears and pain, met mine. "No one did. Morella didn't want *anyone* to know. And, well . . . I didn't either."

I found a chair and sat down, Sushi in my lap now.

He was saying, "A long time ago, I had an affair on a buying trip out of state. It was during a rocky period in my marriage. But the woman never told me she'd got pregnant! I never even saw her again." A rough hand wiped away a tear. "Then, about . . . two years ago . . . Morella showed up on my doorstep saying her mother recently told her I was her father. A DNA test showed that was true."

"And Morella began making demands of you."

Wally shook his head slowly. "Not really. At first I thought she might make trouble—my wife would never have forgiven me if she found out—but all Morella wanted was a little help, which I gladly offered, as best as I could."

"Did your wife know about the weekly cash?"

"I do the books here, so no. And Stella always thought the upstairs could bring in some extra cash as an apartment and was in favor of renting it out."

I asked, "Why do you think Morella came looking for you? She didn't seem to want people to know you were related. Was she running away from something?"

His bushy eyebrows went up. "I don't really know. Morella didn't talk much about her life before coming here."

"But this *new* life in Antiqua didn't seem to suit her, did it? She seems to've always been complaining about it."

"Yeah," he agreed. "She got bored real quick with small-town life."

We fell silent for a moment.

"I'm sorry I caused you pain," I said. "I won't say anything about your relationship to Morella . . . except to the sheriff, of course."

And when it came to something like this, Mother could be trusted not to be an Amy or a Jessica. Or her usual self.

"I'd appreciate that," he said. "I hope Sheriff Borne catches whoever did that terrible thing to my . . . my daughter."

"Trust me," I said. "She will."

Wally nodded. He was working to hold back more tears. Then he blurted, "Oh! What's going on with the mayor? I hear he's gone AWOL."

I smiled. "No, he's turned up. He's fine."

"Good to hear."

Wally's response seemed genuine enough. And for now, I didn't think he needed the details. Mother would have to say how that should be played.

I left, and once again went back outside into the heat.

Just because Wally was Morella's biological father didn't rule out him hitting her in some fit of rage; if he'd hit her unintentionally hard, and thought she was dead, he could have panicked and hidden her in the sarcophagus. Then—believing Myron was his daughter's lover—he might have taken revenge on the mayor, serving up some Poe-etic justice.

My thoughts were interrupted by noises from the next block over—an altercation?

I headed that way. In the street, just outside Top Drawer, two men were fighting, really going at it—one slender, the other burly—like a bar brawl gotten out of hand.

Three guesses who was trying to break it up . . .

. . . .and the first two don't count.

It was Mother, of course.

"Gentlemen!" she said, "Please! Fisticuffs are never a suitable method of settling a dispute!"

When the slender guy shoved her, Sushi jumped from my arms, ran like a jackrabbit, and flung herself onto the man.

I sighed.

What more could possibly happen?

A Trash 'n' Treasures Tip

If a pristine book is what you desire, but beyond your price range, consider buying one of lesser value and condition. You may be able to trade it later for a better one, upgrading over time. Another possibility is a second (or even later) edition from the first issue, having the same book jacket and inner book save for a "first printing" designation on the indicia page. Some book club editions have the same book jacket and typesetting within as the first editions—Rex Stout novels, for example, can be had in their original form for a fraction of the collector's price. My favorite collectible book is *The Message in the Hollow Oak*, Nancy Drew #12 by Carolyn Keene, a 1962 edition of a book copyright 1935. So there!

Chapter Seven

Poe Tableau

Vivian here once again, that is, Sheriff Vivian J. Borne. Things seem to be getting a little gloomy, don't you think, what with all this grisly murder in the air? I think a little levity might be in order—do you agree? Good! We're all due some respite from this steady diet of murder and mayhem.

Here are some truisms I've discovered while traversing the highways and byways of life:

1. Never ask a person older than seventy how they're feeling, because they will probably tell you.
2. Calories in food eaten over the sink while doing the dishes don't count.
3. Housework won't kill you. But why take the chance?
4. Have the wisdom to know, ahead of time, that your skills do not include wallpapering.
5. Accentuate the positives. Medicate the negatives.

This is a joke I recently heard around the water cooler at the county jail. It's a little risqué but will not likely of-fend my readers, who are sophisticated and seasoned in the ways of the world. Just in case, however, I'll leave the telling by utilizing my much-admired upper-crust British accent, which admittedly you won't be able to hear—except on the audio book—but you can *think* it as you read.

(British accent, remember!) There were several elderly chaps who wanted to give their widowed mate (as in friend, not spouse) a present for his eightieth birthday. So they hired a lady of the evening to go to the man's flat. The birthday boy opened the door to find, standing there, a voluptuous (as in Page Three Girl) lass—I mean, bird.

" 'lo gov," she said, out of breath. "Blimey! You sure could use a lift in this place." (Elevator, not spirits—but that, too!)

"What can I do for you, young lady?" he asked.

She purred, "It's what *I* can do for *you*, you lucky bloke."

He queried, "Whatever do you mean, miss?"

And she said, "Your mates 'ave sent me 'round to give you *super sex*."

The gentleman thought a moment, then replied, "I believe I'll have the soup."

Isn't that cute?

Back to the unpleasantness at hand. (You may cease with imagining my British accent—unless you really enjoy it.)

After Caroline Hatcher hauled her husband home, I lingered at the church, waiting for Serenity PD forensics to arrive. Brandy had returned to our Pullman to check on Sushi, who had no doubt been waiting patiently to be put outside. Having a housebroken pet is such a pleasure!

The pastor and I moved to the back of the church and sat together in the last pew, where I took the opportunity to question the man of the cloth further, since Brandy had advised me not to discount him as a suspect.

I asked, conversationally, "I understand you don't much care for the annual E. A. Poe Days."

"Frankly, no," he said. "I find it most distasteful."

"How so?"

He studied me a moment. "It's a profane display. As I told your daughter, lionization of that man and his degenerate works is an offense in the sight of God."

"I see." I chose my next words carefully (but then I choose all of my words carefully). "Do you dislike the event enough to ever do something about it?"

He looked at me with open irritation. "Enough to perhaps wall up one of my parishioners in the basement of my church?" The pastor granted me a small, forgiving smile. "No. I hold the sixth commandment above all else."

" 'Thou shalt not kill,' " I said. "One of my favorites." I changed the subject. "Am I right in assuming that you live in the parsonage behind the church?"

"That's right."

"Alone?"

"Yes." His voice tightened. "I was married once, but . . . well, this life of sacrifice just didn't suit her."

I nodded. "How much of the church can you see from the parsonage?"

He glanced at me curiously. "In the winter, quite a bit, when the trees are bare. Not so much now, with the leaves full."

"Would car headlights pulling into the church draw your attention?"

He considered that. "Occasionally they do. From time to time, I've had to go out and check if anyone was doing mischief."

"And last night?"

"I'd gone to bed by ten. And, again, the trees are full with leaves this time of year."

I moved on. "How *is* attendance here?"

"Good. Well . . . could be better, always. But good."

"And the members, their tithing keeps you afloat?"

"They give what they can." He shrugged. "The whole town is hurting financially, you know."

I was discovering that. "Is the mayor as popular as his wife seems to think?"

He paused, then said, "Well, what man in his position hasn't ruffled a few feathers? But as a whole, Myron *is* well liked. He's been a regular at Sunday services, and a faithful member of the congregation . . . when others of his standing have found more prosperous churches to attend, in surrounding towns. I don't think he'd mind my telling you that he's spearheaded the basement renovation, sometimes supervising the work himself."

He'd recently gotten a little too close a look, hadn't he?

"So," I said, "he would have a key to the church?"

A quick laugh. "No need. The doors here are left unlocked, day and night. The house of God is open to any suffering soul who needs comfort . . . or salvation—no matter the hour."

"That seems awfully trusting, coming from a man of God who has such strong views about 'evil.'"

Pastor Creed gestured with an open hand. "Perhaps, but frankly, what's there to take? Look around, Sheriff. And as for my office, there's nothing of value. Who would want a ten-year-old computer? Vandalism is always a risk, but we've had little of that."

I shifted on the hard pew. "Was Mike Everhart a member here?"

"Yes. Both he and his wife, Lottie. Oh, they didn't attend regularly—Easter, Christmas, a few other times in-between. But they're members."

"Did Mike ever come to you for counsel?"

I perceived a stiffening in the pastor's posture. "Spiritual?"

"Marital."

He tasted his mouth and didn't seem to care for the flavor. "I'm not a gossip, Sheriff, nor do I divulge the private conversations between me and my flock."

"Oh, I understand. It's a bit like the confessional the Catholics have."

He nodded, his body relaxing.

"But," I said, "tell me this, would you? Did you ever sit down with Mike, after the sale of the Poe portrait became public? Post Poe Folly? His eventual suicide indicates he was suffering."

Creed nodded. "I went to see Mike at his store, to offer him comfort because . . . as you indicate . . . I was aware that he would likely be upset."

"And is that how you found him—upset?"

"He obviously was, but he didn't want to talk about it. Just wouldn't open up. Still, I certainly didn't think the man would . . ."

"Take his own life."

"Yes. I failed him."

"You tried. Anyway, more than the embarrassment, and financial loss, of that picture could have been weighing him down."

The pastor, who only sporadically had met my eyes, looked at me now, steadily. "I would say that's fair. Thank you."

Through the windows I could see the forensics utility van drive into the parking lot and come to a stop. Two men got out wearing blue jumpsuits with Serenity PD markings. After thanking him for his time, I left the pastor alone in the pew and went outside to meet the team.

The van's rear double doors were open, revealing metal

shelves along each side, neatly loaded with equipment, some in closed plastic tubs, others in suitcases: fingerprint kit, camera devices, trace evidence kit, bodily fluid collection kit, and containers with such essentials as evidence markers, evidence bags, measuring devices, and personal protective equipment such as gloves, booties, and masks.

As I approached, Wilson—younger of the pair—said ruefully, "This trip is gettin' a little old, Sheriff. I'm starting to feel like I'm commuting."

Wilson was dark-complected with a shaved head, flat nose, and sharp eyes that didn't miss much.

His partner, Henderson—overweight, with salt-and-pepper hair and a world-weary face—quipped, "Maybe we should just book rooms at the motel. What's going on in this town, anyway?"

"I'm not sure, gentlemen," I replied honestly. "I'm hoping you can shed some light on what are starting to look like weirdly staged crimes."

I brought the pair up to speed on the ordeal Mayor Hatcher had survived, filling them in on the Poe aspects that might tie Morella's murder in with the attempted one on Myron. I also informed the specialists of the two workmen, their truck and tools, and the movements of Brandy, Pastor Creed, and myself inside and outside the church.

Wilson worked the perimeter around the back while Henderson took the cellar; for the next hour, I went between them wearing protective blue booties, watching as they worked (I was watching, not the booties).

Henderson grumbled about the cellar area being so compromised he doubted anything substantial would come from his efforts. Since he would find the proximity around the mayor's car similarly spoiled, I decided not to bring the subject up.

Wilson, however, provided an interesting analysis of his

cordoned-off patch: The only tire tracks he could find belonged to the workmen's truck.

Which raised an interesting question: What assailant would park his car in the gravel lot of the church and carry an unconscious man around to the back? Someone not wishing to leave tracks on the earth? Someone who had a helper? Were we looking for more than one perp?

Suddenly the list of suspects expanded to include the workmen.

My cell phone rang—or rather played: the *Hawaii Five-O* theme, which was my new ringtone as sheriff (replacing the frisky piano opening number of *Murder, She Wrote*).

"Sheriff," Myron Hatcher's voice said, "Caroline's taking me to city hall in about half an hour to hand out the last cryptogram."

"Are you sure you're up to it, dear?"

"Very much so."

"Splendid. Don't let the bad guys win! I'll meet you over there. And mayor? The two men who've been working in the cellar—who hired them?"

"Why, I did. They've done jobs for me on my house—a father-and-son operation."

"You're on good terms with the men?"

Surprise registered in his voice. "Well, yes. Why do you ask?"

"I wondered if they might have any grudge against you." Silence. "Mayor, are you still there?"

". . . I did have an issue with some work on the house that I found unsatisfactory. We're still disputing the bill. Frankly, that's why I threw the church job their way, as a kind of peace offering. A goodwill gesture."

"Ah," I said. "Helpful to know. See you shortly."

I replaced my cell on my duty belt.

This seemed a possible lead. Yet a dispute over a bill

didn't seem like much of a murder motive. Why kill the goose before collecting any golden eggs?

And what connection to Morella could the two workers have? Had one been a boyfriend, maybe?

I informed Henderson and Wilson where I was headed, then hoofed it over to city hall. *What I need in my life,* I thought, *is a moped. . . .*

A crowd had gathered in the late afternoon heat, divided into two groups on either side of the front door. Inside, council members Paula, Lottie, Wally, and Rick were milling around the front desk, where the slips of paper were stacked and ready to be distributed. All hands on deck.

Upon seeing me, Paula came forward. "Any word from Myron?"

"He'll be here any minute," I said, watching her face and the others.

The reactions were similar—apparent relief. The exception was Rick, whose expression suggested apathy.

Lottie asked, "Well, Sheriff, what *happened,* anyway?"

"The mayor fell asleep in his shop all night," I said, relying on my acting skills to sell the lie. It was the story Myron and I had agreed upon.

"But," Paula said, frowning in confusion, "I *checked* inside."

Wally, next to her, grunted sarcastically, "Apparently not everywhere."

She shot him a dirty look.

I inquired about just how the last clue would be given out, concerned about crowd control.

Lottie said, "When Myron arrives, we all go outside and hand out the slips with the encrypted clue. Five minutes later, we distribute the unencrypted version."

"Shouldn't it be the other way around?" I asked. "If I'd shelled out ten simoleons, I'd want *my* clue first."

Rick smirked. "We tried that at the first fest, and the folks with the encrypted paper just followed the ones who knew where to go."

Lottie was nodding. "Yesterday, with the first clue, we waited fifteen minutes before handing out the unencrypted version. On the second clue, we waited ten minutes. Today it's only five because so many of the players will've figured out how to decode it themselves."

I said, "Sounds like the festival has been a learning experience."

"Including," Paula said, "learning to get the cash up front for the last clue. Now we have the procedure down for the future."

After this murderous weekend, I doubted there would be any future Edgar Allan Poe Days.

The city hall door opened and Myron Hatcher stepped in, followed closely by Caroline.

The mayor, in a pale blue polo shirt, tan slacks, and brown loafers, was impeccably groomed and looked darn near refreshed; Caroline, however, appeared haggard, her pink cotton dress wrinkled, as if *she* had been the one walled up in the church basement.

Myron smiled broadly at his compatriots as they gathered around him, talking over one another.

"You sure gave us a scare," Paula scolded.

Lottie said, "What good is a cell phone if you don't answer it!"

Actually, the mayor's cell phone had proved very useful, hadn't it?

Rick grumbled, "You owe us *big time* for covering for you at noon."

Wally's "Glad you're okay" seemed obviously halfhearted.

Myron replied, "Sorry to have worried you, folks," and

then clapped his hands. "Now, everyone—back into the fray!"

Paula, Lottie, Wally, and Rick grabbed stacks of the en-crypted clue and filed outside onto the sidewalk. Caroline and I followed, empty-handed, taking positions from which we could monitor the crowd's faces for signs of surprise or alarm at His Honor being alive and well.

But when the mayor made his appearance, joining the others to help pass out the first wave of papers, I spotted no alarmed reaction. These faces all seemed focused on the game that was afoot.

Then the mass disbursed.

Inside, I spoke to Myron about the lack of any reaction among the players to his showing up alive and well.

"The person responsible may not be one of them," he said with a frustrated shrug. "Does that at least help thin the suspect list?"

"Not really," I said. "We might just have a cool cus-tomer out there playing his or her own game. Anyway, maniacs don't necessarily react as they should. I mean—they're maniacs!"

In five minutes, the passing-out clues process (unen-crypted this time) was repeated for the paying customers, who flew up the street in the direction of Top Drawer An-tiques.

Myron said, "I'd better go help our clerk, Ryan—that poor kid'll be overwhelmed! Coming, Caroline?"

"I'll be along, dear. I want to have a word with the sheriff."

He gave his wife a peck on the cheek and left.

Paula, Lottie, Wally, and Rick also departed to tend to their shops, even though they would probably not be very busy.

Alone with Caroline, I asked, "Did *you* see anyone act-ing suspiciously?"

She shook her head. "No, other than all of them are lunatics, playing this stupid game."

I could only nod.

Then her hand was on my arm. "Sheriff, how much danger do you think Myron is in?"

"I don't think it's likely," I said, "that there will be a repeat performance of what happened to your husband."

"Not likely, you say—but it could happen?"

"Well, anything could, but I doubt any elaborate Poe nonsense would be mounted. But a more old-fashioned murder is a possibility."

"Oh my Lord!"

"But two things will soon improve your husband's chances." I raised a forefinger. "One, the outsiders will be gone soon after the prize is found . . . and if the killer is one of them, or using them for cover, that's good for Myron." Although not good for me in solving this mystery. I offered a second finger. "Two, Serenity's chief of police is arriving tonight."

"You called him in?" Caroline asked.

"No. Brandy did. He and my daughter are, as the French say, *les amoureux*."

More or less amour, depending on how things were going.

Caroline's frown said she'd lost me in translation. "Well," she said, "whatever your daughter and the chief are, it will be comforting to have more law enforcement professionals on hand."

I had mixed emotions about that myself, but I knew it would comfort her. I was not looking forward to having Tony Cassato looking over my shoulder, second-guessing me and treating me as less than a real "law enforcement professional," even though I'd solved far more murders than he ever had.

After Caroline departed, I was left alone with my

thoughts, which I admit can make for disturbing company. My theatrically attuned mind was going over all of the possibilities for Poe-themed murders that might lay ahead. Was someone planning to pluck the heart from a victim's body and bury it beneath the floorboards? Had an unknown fiend out there dug a pit and polished up a pendulum?

I needed to distract my thoughts and quench my thirst, so I wandered down the hallway toward the back, where I located a small lunchroom with a Coca-Cola vending machine. Scrutinizing the drinks, I did not see what I wanted. As usual.

Irritated, I took out my cell phone, looked up an e-mail address on the net, then, thumbs flying, wrote the following:

Dear President of the Coca-Cola Company,
Why don't you ever stock TAB in your machines? If your reasoning is that it's fallen out of favor, whose fault is that? Don't you realize there are 76.4 million boomers, flush with retirement cash (some at least), who were weaned on the drink? We want diet sodas, sure, but not ones that scream "diet," reminding us that we're overweight. We already know that!

So take some money and make a commercial, and run it in key spots, like during *Jeopardy!*, for instance. We've had enough advertisements about blood thinners, adult diapers, and colon cancer test kits! We want to be reminded of our youth, not the rocky path to the beyond. There are plenty of famous "seasoned" actors you could use who still look good (just don't shoot them with an HD camera!).

Here's an idea for a commercial you can have for free (I'll sign off on it): Open with an old-fashioned county fair, the midway, coming in for a semi-close-up of Diane Keaton/Lane or Jessica Lange, or Sally Field who's also held up nicely (Meryl Streep might be over even Coke's budgetary range, as she's a three-time Oscar winner). Cut to a medium shot of a well-preserved male actor like Kevin Costner or Pierce Brosnan or Jeff Bridges (Denzel Washington would be a bold choice!) who hands her a TAB, BUT make sure he also has one himself, so it's not like a "Here, you're fat, so take this" kind of thing. Music is important. Might I suggest "Do You Believe in Magic" by the Lovin' Spoonful, or "Good Vibrations" by the Beach Boys ($$$$), or something for the old stoners like Steppenwolf's "Magic Carpet Ride" (I'm sitting on the fence about legalizing marijuana; two legs swung over on the "no" side. But I'm okay with it used medically.)

(**Note to Vivian from Editor:** Must I scold you once again?)

(**Note to Editor from Vivian:** Sorry—I am just reporting what occurred.)

I saved my e-mail to finish later, then walked back out front, pondering what to do with myself next. Suddenly, distant shouting reached my ears—anyway, my good ear—drawing my attention out the windows.

I had a decent view of the next block, where two men—one reminding me somewhat of George Carlin, the other Ernest Borgnine, the middle-aged variety of both—were having an altercation on the sidewalk in front of Top Drawer Antiques. A crowd was gathering, building, watching; Myron was among them, looking on mortified.

As the combatants moved out into the street, I left city hall on the run—perhaps better described as a jog, or let's call it a power walk. My light duty belt had neither gun nor Taser (let alone shark repellent, like Adam West's Batman) but did contain a small can of Mace, which I could use to break up what had now become a full-fledged fight.

Pushing through the crowd on the periphery, the can of Mace in one hand, I reached the pair of whirling dervishes.

What are whirling dervishes, you may wonder. Well, reader mine, they are members of a Turkish order of Sufis dating back to the twelfth century, whose ritual consisted partially of a highly stylized whirling dance. The expression is used today to describe anyone who has abundant energy and is not considered derogative in anyway.

(**Brandy to Mother:** Get on with it!)

I yelled, as if to the back row of the Playhouse, "Stop in the name of the law!"

I don't know for sure which of the pair pushed me, but I stumbled backward, the Mace tumbling from my hand; only barely did I manage to stay upright.

Suddenly Sushi appeared, a whirling dervish herself, attacking George Carlin, then the *McHale's Navy* captain, her claws scratching, sharp little teeth biting at whoever and wherever she could. The little beast scampering and clawing and nipping proved too much of a distraction for the combatants.

The fighting ceased.

"You're both under arrest," I declared, feet steady under me now.

Carlin and Borgnine glared at each other.

Myron, at my side, said, "They were fighting over this." He held out the Poe *Tales* book.

Carlin snapped, "I got to it first!"

"He's *lying!*" growled Borgnine.

Sushi growled too, down by my feet now. Yup (as Gary Cooper said), this would be the last Edgar Allan Poe fest, all right.

"Quiet you two," I ordered them. Then to the mayor I said, "I'll need your conference room for my interrogation, that is, *interview*."

"Is that necessary?" His Honor asked, frowning. "I *saw*

what happened. My clerk Ryan, too. We could settle it right here."

"I'm afraid not. I'll need the men's statements . . . and yours and Ryan's."

Myron sighed. "Okay. We'll close up, then join you." He held out the book. "Do you want to hold on to this, Sheriff? As evidence, maybe?"

I took the prize.

(**Brandy to Mother:** I'll say.)

Turning back to Carlin and Borgnine, I commanded, "Come with me, gentlemen. Any more trouble out of you and I slap you both in handcuffs."

I had only one set of cuffs, but what they didn't know couldn't hurt me.

Brandy appeared at my side, with Sushi in her arms now. "Are you all right, Mother?" she asked.

I whispered, "Please, dear—*Sheriff*." Then, full voice, as if I didn't mind being overheard (which I didn't), I said, "It takes more than a little shove to put Vivian Borne out of commission!"

Then whispering again, I said to her, "Where have you *been,* darling girl? Never mind—I need you as a witness. And you never know when Sushi's teeth might come in handy again."

Shortly, six people and a canine were seated in the cool confines of city hall's conference room. I was at one end of the table, Carlin to my right, Myron next to him, then pudgy young Ryan of the cherubic visage. To my left, across from Carlin, sat Borgnine, and beside him, Brandy with Sushi (that last sounds a bit like an order in a Japanese restaurant, doesn't it?).

From a pouch I removed a tiny tape recorder, which I positioned on the table in front of me, turned on, and said, "Sheriff Vivian Borne," then gave the date and location.

I gave Carlin a steely-eyed look. "What is your name?"

"John Miller."

"From?"

"St. Louis, Missouri."

"Business?"

"Antiques dealer."

I looked at Borgnine. "And you?"

He was more forthcoming. "Paul Oldfield, Morris, Illinois. I'm a construction worker, but my wife runs an antiques shop. She couldn't come to the festival herself, so she sent me to try to land the Poe prize."

Back to John Miller. "What's *your* story?"

He shrugged. "I spotted the book on top of a curio cabinet, got to it first, and this clown grabbed it out of my hands."

"That's a *lie!*" Oldfield exclaimed. "*He* snatched it out of *my* hands."

"Quiet," I said to Borgnine, I mean, Oldfield. "You'll have your turn. Go on, Mr. Miller."

"Well, I tried to take the book back, and it fell on the floor, and we started to . . . you know, scuffle some."

I looked at Oldfield. "You're up."

"*I* had the book first, and he wrenched it out of my hands. He's lucky he didn't damage it. So I . . . I punched him. In self-defense. I mean, he got rough first."

"Mayor Hatcher," I said, "what say you?"

Myron took a deep breath. "Well, I'd arrived back at the shop from handing out the final clue, when I saw this gentleman"—he nodded at Miller—"take the book from the top of the cabinet. Then that gentleman"—a nod to Oldfield—"tried to take it away."

Oldfield said, "Now *he's* lying."

I asked, "Mayor, you *saw* Mr. Oldfield grab the book from Mr. Miller?"

"Well, Mr. Oldfield did have his back to me . . . but Mr. Miller had the book in his possession first. That much I can verify. And I am relieved that the book doesn't seem to have been damaged."

I asked Ryan, "Can you corroborate that?"

The chubby young clerk shifted in his chair, then nodded. "Ah, yeah . . . that's what happened."

The construction worker said, pleadingly, "Sheriff, I *swear* I found the book first."

"Mr. Oldfield," I said, "based on what I've just heard, I'm awarding Mr. Miller the book. I suggest you leave Antiqua immediately."

He frowned. "Who put *you* in charge?"

"The good citizens of Serenity County. If you would prefer to remain in Antiqua and face a charge of assault and battery, that can be arranged. If you were to be found innocent, then you could pursue the matter in civil court, and—"

The man stood angrily, pushing back his chair, scraping the floor. "You needn't concern yourself about that! And I'll never come back to this terrible little town again."

Sushi growled and bared her teeth.

Oldfield strode angrily to the doorway, where he paused to look back. "And don't think I won't use social media to tell everybody what a *fraud* this has been!"

He disappeared before I could advise him not to slander anyone.

I put the book on the table, gently, and pushed it the same way toward Miller. "I suggest you leave town as well."

"My room is paid through tomorrow," the antiques dealer said, surprised.

"Well, then, make it first thing in the morning."

"Is that an order, Sheriff?"

"Call it a strongly worded suggestion."

Miller nodded, picked up the book, and rose. "All right, Sheriff. And thank you."

I nodded.

He left.

After I turned off the recorder, the room fell silent, a silence broken when the mayor muttered, "What a debacle. This may be our final Edgar Allan Poe Days."

This thought had occurred to me already, as I've shared with you. Still, the idea of never performing "The Raven" here again was difficult to countenance.

"Nonsense," I said. "Most folks will take Mr. Oldfield's ranting on social media as the sour grapes that they are!"

"I hope you're right, Sheriff," Myron said. "And thank you for handling this unfortunate event so fairly and efficiently." He paused. "If Ryan and I are no longer needed, we should be getting back to the store."

"Go right ahead."

They departed.

Brandy and Sushi moved down to take Miller's empty chair.

"Mother," she said in a low voice, "I have an interesting revelation to share."

"Speak up, dear. My right ear is blocked. By the by, do you think there's any particular difference between wax removal products? The one I tried recently didn't seem to have the proper snap, crackle, and pop."

"Mother!"

"Not *that* loud, dear."

Splitting the difference, she said, "Wally Thorp told me in confidence that he's Morella's biological father."

I sat back and gave a low whistle. "Good heavens. Now some things are beginning to make sense."

"Yeah," Brandy said, "but I still wouldn't rule Thorp out. It's not like Morella was a daughter he'd raised. She was a stranger, the result of a passing fling. The two of them were seen having heated arguments, and he might well have accidentally killed her in one."

I frowned. "Filicide is rare, but it *does* happen. But why would Wally take action against Myron?"

She gave me her theory that Wally may have suspected that his daughter was having an affair with the mayor.

I looked at Brandy with newfound admiration. "Interesting."

My cell phone sang its Hawaiian song. The caller was Ben Saukenuk, manager of the Tomahawk.

"Sheriff Borne," he said, "I have that information you requested—footage showing the Crafton woman's cell phone."

My pulse quickened. "Including the number of her caller?"

"Yes. Would you like to come see the footage?"

"Just give me the phone number, please."

He did, and I wrote it down.

I thanked him, then instructed the casino manager to hold on to that footage, as it would be needed as evidence.

Cell phone numbers—and landlines as well—could be accessed through the sheriff's car computer, but that meant a hike back to the Explorer parked at the church.

I didn't want to wait that long, so I found out the old-fashioned way: by calling the number myself.

A voice I recognized as Lottie Everhart's answered.

"You have reached City Hall. If you know your party's extension, dial it now. Otherwise, please leave a brief message and phone number, and someone will get back to you. Thank you, and have a nice day!"

I stood, then hurried through the hallway to the front desk. A blinking on the answering machine made a small beacon to light my way, keeping my investigation off the rocks, guiding me toward the port of justice. (I think that was a splendid metaphor, don't you?)

(**Note to Vivian from Editor:** *No.*)

The list of suspects had suddenly narrowed to those

who had a key to city hall to use the phone Thursday night—Lottie, Paula, Wally, and Rick.

Vivian's Trash 'n' Treasures Tip

Most rare books are old, so expect some wear and tear. Reputable book dealers will describe these flaws; if they don't, don't buy the book, or return it for a refund. But if you do keep the book, don't try to fix it with Scotch invisible tape . . . which isn't all that invisible.

Chapter Eight

Poe, Poe, Poe Your Boat

Brandy back in charge. Or, anyway, back.

Saturday evening, Mother and I were seated in the air-conditioned parlor of the Pullman, enjoying soothing cups of hot tea, when a sharp knock came at the door, startling us just a little—Sushi, too, curled up between us.

"Entrée!" Mother called out.

The door opened and the chief of the Serenity PD police, one Tony Cassato, strode in like he owned the place. Of course this guy owned any place he strode into—late forties, graying temples, steely gray eyes, square jaw, thick neck, barrel chest.

Tony was not in his standard work attire of light blue shirt, navy tie, tan slacks, and brown Florsheims, most likely because technically he was not on duty. But I was mildly amused that he had maintained a similar conservative look by way of a blue short-sleeved polo shirt, tan shorts, and brown slip-ons, sans socks.

Readers who are familiar with our disjointed and sometimes dysfunctional courtship may skip down to the paragraph beginning, "Sushi, seeing Tony, went bananas." All others continue on.

Tony arrived in Serenity about four years ago from the East Coast to take our local top-cop position, a duty that soon found him butting heads with Mother thanks to her interference in a murder case (*Antiques Roadkill*). Being her (often unwitting and unwilling) cohort in crime, I also got off to a rocky start with Tony. Gradually, however, we warmed to each other, and he came to understand (if not accept) that, due to Mother's bipolar disorder, my loyalty must always tilt in her already tilted direction.

For a long time, Tony was a man of mystery. Then, one evening at his cabin where we were . . . let's call it enjoying each other's company . . . an assassin came calling (*Antiques Knock-Off*). A Mafia godfather had taken a contract out on the chief, who had testified against a certain crime family in New Jersey. After we managed to escape, Tony suddenly disappeared out of my life and into WITSEC (witness protection).

Later, on a trip that Mother and I took to New York City to attend a comic book convention (*Antiques Con*), Mother (unbeknownst to me) paid the mob's elderly godfather a visit and convinced him to drop the contract (the baked ziti she brought may have been a factor, along with helping him solve a literal family problem).

Which brought Tony back into my life, both personally and locally. Since then we've had two more bumps in the road: the appearance in Serenity of his estranged wife, whom he thought had divorced him after he signed the papers she'd never filed (*Antiques Frame*), and most recently Mother running for, and becoming, the sheriff of Serenity County (*Antiques Wanted*). The first bump was settled; the second . . . we'll have to see.

It's a good thing all of that is true, or it might sound ridiculous.

Sushi, seeing Tony, went bananas, whimpering, leaping up at our visitor's bare legs (so glad those nails were clipped recently!), demanding to be picked up—which Tony did—and then she sniffed everywhere she could take her nose. While Sushi was very fond of Tony, she was fonder of his dog, Rocky (*not* named for our relationship), and his scent on the chief was like catnip, if the dog were a cat, which of course she wasn't.

Still with me?

Mother asked regally, "Care for some tea, my good man?"

Tea always brought out the English accent in her. My quick frown sent it packing.

Tony peeled Sushi off and set her on the floor. "No, thanks. But should you have a cold *beer* . . ."

Having thoughtfully stocked Tony's brand (Busch) in the little fridge, I left to fetch one.

I returned and handed the cold sweating can to the chief, who was seated rather absurdly on a much-too-small-for-him velvet chair. Sushi was spread out on the rug, tummy down, spent from her fuss over Tony.

Tony started right in. "Your reading of the crime scene, Vivian, was spot-on—blunt force trauma, the unconscious girl shut in that sarcophagus. She wakes up, suffocating, tries to claw her way out—unsuccessfully. Obviously."

"Terrible," Mother said, for once shaken by the reality of death. "Is there any reason to keep this information under wraps, Chief?"

"No," he said simply.

Without preamble, Mother shared *her* new info. "Because the call Morella received at the casino came from a city hall landline, my list of suspects has narrowed to the council members?"

"Uptalking," I said to her.

Mildly flustered, she said, "Sorry. At any rate, I feel I

should round up the council immediately, rather than wait till morning."

Her pause indicated that she was open to Tony's opinion. He was kind enough not to point out that "immediately" had not happened yet, though cups of tea for Mother and her sort-of-deputy had.

Instead he said, diplomatically, "It's your show."

Mother smiled, liking that. Which was probably why she said next, "Perhaps you could attend the group interview—not in any official capacity, of course, but as another seasoned set of eyes and ears."

"Of course," he said with a nod.

What was his game?

As Mother sat on the couch using her cell phone to call the council members and have them meet her at city hall, I led Tony back to the galley kitchen.

I said, "You're being awfully nice to her."

He shrugged. "She's the county sheriff, I'm the city chief of police. We need to get along. Cooperate. Respect each other."

"You respect Mother?"

"She has a nose for sniffing out murderers. I'll give her that."

I stood close to him, put my arms around him. "I'm so glad you're here," I whispered.

"I am too. Getting gladder by the second."

My eyes held his. "She needs your help, you know, but won't ask for it. And if you step in and take over, it'll just make things worse."

Worse for me, I was thinking.

Tony nodded. "You may think I'm just a big lug, but I do have a certain . . ."

"Finesse?"

"Damn straight. You said on the phone she was making reckless decisions. Care to elaborate?"

I shook my head, my eyes leaving his. "No."

"Why not?"

"Because then you'd have to do something about it."

"Ah. I see."

I pursed my lips. "Tony, this is her first big test as sheriff, and Mother wants to do well. She knows she has a certain . . . not finesse, but reputation. And wants people to think well of her in this new role."

His smile was a sideways thing. "Brandy, if she doesn't stay within the law, she'll have a lot more to worry about than what people think." He lifted my chin with a finger, looked into my eyes. "Look, I'll be around until this is resolved, and help where she'll let me . . . or work behind the scenes when she won't."

I nodded. "You'll cover her behind?"

"Consider it covered. And I'll throw yours in for free. Feel better?"

I nodded. "Way better."

He sighed. "Me too."

About half an hour later, Mother, Tony, and I were greeted in front of city hall by the mayor himself, the first to arrive at Mother's impromptu summons. I introduced Tony, and the two men shook hands.

"I hope this is important, Sheriff," Myron said with a tinge of irritation. "Caroline and I were in the middle of a late dinner." He'd downgraded his country-club clothes to shorts and a short-sleeve shirt.

"Important," she said, "is exactly what it is."

Myron's eyes went to Tony, apparently hoping the Serenity chief might elaborate on his presence, but neither he nor Mother enlightened the mayor.

Inside city hall, Myron turned on the lights, and we headed down the corridor to the conference room, where more lights were switched on.

Mother moved to the head of the table and sat there,

Myron taking a chair next to her. Tony and I stood down at the opposite end of the room, in front of a medium-sized green chalkboard on the wall.

No one said anything.

Next to arrive was an agitated Rick, in cutoff jeans, T-shirt, and thongs.

"What's the deal? I'm trying to relax after a crazy-hard day." He yanked out a chair next to Myron and plopped into it. Not everybody can sit down angrily—it's a gift.

Then came Wally, looking sleepy and in typically disheveled attire. "I don't appreciate being woken up, so this better be good." He sank down in the chair next to Rick.

Paula and Lottie arrived together, the former in gray sweatshirt and pants, the latter in an off-the-shoulder blouse and short-shorts, fully made-up and hair coiffed.

With a smirk, Paula said to Mother, "You're lucky I hadn't taken my sleeping pill yet."

She joined Wally. Lottie said nothing, dutifully taking the chair on the end, near Tony and me.

Mother Hen addressed her chicks all in a row. "Thank you for coming at this hour at such short notice." She gestured to Tony. "This is Chief Anthony Cassato from the Serenity Police Department."

The council swiveled their heads toward Tony, then back to Mother, who said, "His presence is not official, as he just happened to be attending the festival. But since he was available, I've asked him here to advise and consult."

The council members exchanged frowning glances, mixing a cocktail of confusion and irritation.

"I think it's time to set aside a certain little white lie," Mother said.

Eyes all around the table widened.

"Myron," she continued, "did not fall asleep in his shop last night. He was attacked around midnight. About to get into his car, he was hit on the head, then conveyed to the church, where he was walled up unconscious in the basement. With bricks. His hands were secured, his mouth stuffed with a gag. Fortunately, I found him in time."

The reaction was swift—and predictable.

"Oh my God!" Lottie gasped, a hand going to her ample chest.

"Thank goodness you're all right!" Paula said to Myron, adding with just a little irritation, "So I *hadn't* overlooked you."

Wally asked, "What does this mean?"

Rick provided an uncalled-for answer: "It means this stupid Poe festival has attracted some psychopathic killer! And what are you going to *do* about it, Sheriff? Not that you're in any way qualified!"

Mother looked at the young man, who sneered at her and leaned back arrogantly in his chair.

She said to him, "I'll begin with a question, Mr. Wheeler. Where were *you* last night between eleven and two?"

"What?" Rick blurted. "You're nuttier than a Salted Nut Roll if you think I, or any *one* of us, would do such a thing to Myron!"

Heads nodded in agreement, accompanied by muttering.

"Two things," Mother said. "First, it may not have been one of you. It might have been *two* of you."

The objections to that overlapped into an unintelligible cacophony.

"And second," Mother said, "answer my question, Mr. Wheeler. Where *were* you?"

Grudgingly, Rick said, "At home. Asleep."

"Alone?"

"Alone! Not the best alibi, I guess."

"Not the best, I would agree."

Mother went down the line asking every one of them

the same question. Paula, Wally, and Lottie's responses were similar to Rick's, to say the least. Paula had taken her usual sleeping pill, Wally slept in his recliner all night, and Lottie watched a late movie and then went to bed.

Everyone in Antiqua seemed to sleep alone. At least on the city council. Even *Myron* had slept alone, hadn't he? Walled up in that church basement.

And of course, any one of them could have left their homes and attacked the mayor.

"The time has come," Mother said portentously, and for a moment I thought she'd continue with: *To talk of many things: of shoes—and ships—and sealing-wax—of cabbages—and kings . . .*

Thankfully she just filled them in, straightforward, on the grisly reality of Morella's death, which needed poetry from neither Poe nor Lewis Carroll.

Only Mother and I knew that Wally was the late young woman's father, and he showed no obvious emotion. But I could see a slight trembling and dampening eyes.

A clearly shaken Lottie asked, "Sheriff, do you think what happened to Morella and Myron was the work of the same person?"

"Likely," Mother replied.

"Then it has to be someone who came to Poe Days," Lottie reasoned. "Like Rick said—some *psycho!*"

"But why pick on us?" Wally grumbled, seeming put-upon by the very thought of murder.

Mother leaned forward, elbows on the table, tenting her fingers. "I was just about to come to that."

"Well, get on with it," Rick snapped. "We were *already* tired—now we're scared silly, too!"

(He didn't say "silly"—he used the kind of word that keeps a book out of Walmart.)

Mother cocked her head. "I feel quite well rested, Mr.

Wheeler, thank you very much . . . and am prepared to stay here all night, if need be. It takes more to scare Vivian Borne than some deranged practical joker."

She could speak for herself. All this sounded plenty scary to the pro bono deputy.

Rick had nothing to say.

Her chick back in line, Mother asked, "Who besides yourselves has a key to this building?"

The seeming non sequitur of a question threw the council off base for a moment.

Then Myron replied. "Well, besides us . . . the treasurer, Bob Stewart, has one, of course."

Mother frowned at the mayor. "I haven't met him. Has Mr. Stewart been around?"

"No," replied Myron. "Bob is in Arizona attending a family funeral. Won't be back until next week."

"I see. Anyone else given a key?"

"The secretary we lost due to budget cuts," Paula offered, then leaned forward to look at the mayor. "Did she ever return it?"

Myron nodded. "Before leaving town for another job. I think all the keys are accounted for."

"No, Pastor Creed has one," Lottie reminded him. "The sanctuary air-conditioning broke down in July, remember? And he held some meetings with church elders here. I don't know if he ever returned that key. Myron?"

The mayor frowned. "He might have. But, frankly, I don't recall that he did."

"All right," Mother said. "Were any of you in city hall on Thursday night between ten and ten-thirty?"

The five council members exchanged puzzled looks, then all shook their heads. It was so well coordinated they might have practiced it.

"Well, *someone* was here that night," Mother told

them. "Someone with a key to get in after hours and use the landline."

Myron asked, "How do you know that?"

"Because that person called Morella Crafton on the city hall line at precisely ten twenty-six. Not long before the young woman was murdered."

The room filled with murmurs as the council looked up and down the line at one another. I watched as faces registered surprise, then—as the weight of Mother's words dragged them down—alarm, and finally suspicion.

Paula, wincing, gestured vaguely around her. "You're saying one of *us* killed Morella?"

"For the moment," Mother said, "I'm making no accusations. Merely stating facts."

Rick stood. "You know what I think? I think you're looking for somebody to pin this on! You're new on the job and want to wrap things up quick, make yourself look good. Well, I'm not going to help you do that. If you have any more questions for me, you'll have to talk my lawyer." He pushed the chair away. "Who else is smart enough to leave with me?"

Wally rose, then Lottie, and Paula, and they all followed Rick out of the conference room. I was reminded of prisoners marching out to break rocks.

Only Myron remained.

Tony and I joined Mother at the table, sitting on either side.

"Of course," Mother said with a sigh, "I didn't expect someone to admit making the call. But I had to try. Had to put it out there."

The mayor's expression seemed almost painfully earnest. "Sheriff, I *know* my fellow council members. They're good people. This festival takes it out of all of them, and now . . . all of this craziness? I think you're going down the wrong road here—someone, *anyone*, could have picked the lock to get in and use our phone."

Mother said, "Yes. But why would they? And even if there was some reason to do so—perchance, to implicate you council members—they would be taking quite a risk. The streets here are well lighted at night, and there's still activity at ten o'clock, especially at the bar."

"But not in the alley," Myron pointed out. "You're assuming this person came in the front door."

"I am," Mother said.

"Why?"

"Because," she said, "the rear of the bank shares that alley, which I bet has motion-detecting flood lights and likely one security camera at least."

Nodding, Tony said, "I believe the sheriff's right. Who would question a council member being in this building at *any* hour? But a council member who wanted to use a phone without being heard or seen would know this line would be safe. Or would have been, were it not for the sheriff's sharp detective work."

Touched by that, Mother said, "Thank you, Chief."

I addressed Myron. "You say you know your council members well . . . but how well do you know Pastor Creed? He dislikes the very idea of the festival, is agitated about the mausoleum not being secured, and now we've learned he probably still has a key to city hall. And I don't think anyone who saw *him* unlock the front door would think much of *that*, either."

The mayor was shaking his head. "No. No. He's a devoutly religious man. He just wouldn't . . . *couldn't* have done such a thing to me. And why would he kill the Crafton girl? How could he even conceive of killing anyone?"

"As an example," I said firmly. "A harsh warning to any locals who'd been using the mausoleum for illicit purposes."

Mother was nodding. "My darling deputy speaks wisely. Pastor Creed could have seen Morella there in the graveyard, which he considered his turf. He may have picked poor Morella as his instrument of retribution."

She paused.

"And you, Mayor—the good pastor might see striking you down for representing this godless festival honoring a degenerate author's evil works, viewing both of these twisted acts of revenge as being for the greater good."

The mayor was frowning, shaking his head. "Pastor Creed *did* voice his displeasure over the festival and the mausoleum at several meetings, but . . ."

"Well, there you go," I said.

"But this just doesn't seem like anything he'd be capable of."

Mother said, "There is one question you can clear up for me, Mayor. How was it that the Poe book was hidden in your store?"

He shrugged. "Sheerly a random matter. We drew for which location. Names of participating businesses were put in a bowl, and mine happened to be picked."

"By whom?" Mother asked.

"Is that important?"

"Possibly."

He thought back. "Well let's see . . . I believe *Paula* drew it out."

"You saw the slip?" Mother asked.

Myron shrugged again. "No, I took her word. Why wouldn't I?"

Mother said nothing.

The mayor frowned. "Why in the world are you asking me about this, Sheriff?"

Mother sidestepped the question and posed one of her own. "Might I ask a favor, Your Honor?"

"Certainly."

She gestured to the chalkboard across the room. "I would like to use that."

Tony and I exchanged tiny smiles. On prior cases Mother had always compiled her suspect list on an old schoolroom blackboard on wheels in our library; she must have felt adrift here without it. Once she even "borrowed" a sandwich chalkboard from a restaurant.

"Sheriff," the mayor said magnanimously, "you may come in here any time you please. If you need one of our famous *keys* . . ."

"No, dear. I want to take it *with* me."

"Take what where?"

"The chalkboard, dear."

"Uh, okay," he replied, puzzled. "If it'll come off the wall."

Almost everything Mother did was off the wall.

"And don't worry," she said, "I'll bring it back. I merely mean to commandeer it for a day or so."

Tony and I stayed around to assist in freeing the chalkboard from its screws, then helped her load it into the rear of the Explorer. Tony played prisoner in the grilled-in backseat while I drove us to the Pullman, where we helped Mother in with her new toy.

After that, Tony and I walked off into a surprisingly nice, cooled-down night to find something to eat. I, for one, had worked up an appetite.

We wound up at the only place in tiny Antiqua where we might get a bite at this late hour—the Happy Hour bar, on the main floor of another old Victorian brick building, across from Wally's store, Junk 'n' Stuff.

The watering hole was hopping on this Saturday night of the biggest weekend of the local year. The tin-ceilinged, wooden-floored establishment had a central open area for dancing to the jukebox and a Long Branch Saloon–style bar with a backing mirror and a lineup of liquor bottles. With Tony in the lead like the prow of a ship, we made our way through happy dancers and happier drinkers to the rear with its small tables and a handful of high-backed booths.

As Tony and I pushed through, I noticed Wally seated at the bar. He saw us, quickly downed a tumbler of golden liquid, and made for the door.

As we neared the back, I mentally asked Yellow Feather— the Native American spirit guide who always gets me good parking places—to expand his powers to bar booths. Suddenly two middle-aged women seated in one such booth vacated it, leaving behind half-filled glasses of red wine. They would soon find themselves outside, wondering what had happened. Thank you, Yellow Feather!

(Or maybe they'd had three glasses and just wanted to go home.)

At any rate, we slid in on opposite sides of the booth, and a barmaid came over. Tony inquired about food. Slices of microwaved mini-pizza were on offer, and not much else, but that sounded gourmet to me about now. Tony ordered sausage and a Busch on tap, and I asked for pepperoni and white Zin.

Earlier, when Tony had told me he could join me at the festival Saturday evening, I had envisioned a romantic dinner with him. But this would have to do.

Anyway, despite the noisy atmosphere, most of the chatter was up front along the bar, and the jukebox was muffled, the high sides of the wooden booth allowing us to talk without raising our voices.

Tony asked, "How are you holding up?"

"Just fine."

His expression revealed I'd flunked his built-in lie detector.

So I sighed and said, "This pro bono deputy gig is harder than I thought it would be."

Why did I say that?

Tony wasn't going to give me any sympathy, not after warning me it was foolish to sign on as Mother's driver. How *else* could I have kept an eye on her? If he was going to berate and belittle me now, I might just get up and walk out. . . .

But Tony said, "I'm here for you, Brandy. Whatever you need."

And I just about cried.

Our little pizzas and drinks arrived, and we talked about other things (cabbages and kings?): that the Cubs were doing so well they could be on their way to another World Series; how he had a bumper crop in his vegetable garden at his cabin needing to be eaten else canned (the vegetables, not the cabin); and whether we should get tickets to a concert series in Des Moines with the Oak Ridge Boys (he liked), Tonic Sol-fa (I liked), and Jackson Browne (we both liked).

My spirits, Native American or otherwise, had lifted considerably by the time our microwave meal was finished, and we were enjoying another round of drinks when Tony's eyes moved from me toward the front of the room. He nodded his head slightly, and I craned for a look.

Rick and Lottie had just come in, Rick muscling up to the bar to order drinks while Lottie gazed around. She spotted us, elbowed Rick; he saw us, and they walked out.

Tony said, "We're popular tonight."

"Second only to Mother."

"Are those two a couple?"

"Maybe. Or just feeling shared guilt about something. . . ."

A little before midnight, we left the bar to stroll along
the main drag, shops shuttered for the night. When we
turned up a side street, past the alley behind the row of antiques stores, I noticed Paula going in the back of her
shop, Relics Antiques, and slowed my pace. In a few moments the upper floor lights of her apartment went on.

I hadn't seen her in the bar. So where had she been for
the past few hours?

The weather had cooled considerably—a welcome relief
from the heat and humidity—and a pleasant breeze kissed
my face. That was almost as good as Tony doing it.

He took my hand as we walked along, discussing—or,
rather, negotiating—how we could make a late summer
fishing excursion to Canada as much fun for non-fisher-
woman me as for rod and reeling him (casting my line at
Mall of America on the way would be a start). Soon we
found ourselves at the park lit only by a half moon.

The picnic tables were empty, as were the log cabin shelters. In the deserted playground, the swings rocked to and
fro, as if inhabited by little ghosts; the wind was picking up.
We proceeded to the bank of the pond, where a single rowboat, broken away from others tethered to a dock across the
water, was banging against the shore in the now-rippling
water.

Tony looked at me. "Shall we return it?"

I smiled and nodded.

On the bank, he steadied the boat while I climbed aboard,
then sat on the rear bench. Then he got in, so graceful for a
big man.

"Take the long way around," I said.

He smiled and took the oars in hand.

I leaned back against the flat stern and gazed up at the

multitude of glittering stars, listening to the soothing and rhythmic sound of the oars as he rowed.

"I wish you had a banjo," I mused, the effects of the second glass of white Zin lingering.

"If I did, I couldn't play it."

"Then sing something."

He frowned. "Have you ever heard me sing?"

"No. But can't be that bad. Come on, be a sport. There's no one here but us chickens."

"What do you want to hear?"

I thought for a moment. "How about 'Down by the Old Mill Stream'?"

"I only know the chorus."

"That'll do."

"Down by the old mill stream where I first met you . . ."

Hey, what do you know? Tony Cassato had a wonderful baritone voice.

"Not bad," I interrupted him. "But put some feeling into it—this is where you first met me, remember? In the song, of course. The love of your life."

He maybe made a face at that, but it was dark, so I couldn't be sure.

"With your eyes of blue, dressed in gingham, too."

I slid down farther, lay my head on the back of the boat.

"It was there I knew that you loved me true."

And trailed a hand in the water.

"You were sixteen, my village queen, by the old mill stream."

How romantic . . .

Something touched my hand, and I yanked it out.

"Got a nibble?" Tony chuckled.

"Maybe," I laughed, feeling silly.

I looked over the edge of the rowboat, down into the black, murky water, and a body popped up.

A Trash 'n' Treasures Tip

Know precisely what you are searching for. Vague memories or partial descriptions of a book are not enough to go on. Have a complete title, the author's name, year the book was printed, and the name of the publisher. Online, I thought I had ordered an inspirational book, *The Road Less Traveled*, but what arrived was a travel book on back-country roads with the same title. I considered sending it back, but Mother was having too much fun reading it. And underlining.

Chapter Nine

Poe Foe

Vivian taking the reign again.

You would-be wordsmiths (and word-joneses for that matter), just look at what I did there! It's a play on words—taking the reins, taking the reign. A little wordplay, even at the most stressful of times, is always welcomed by readers.

Even though I feel—in the writing of these nonfiction true-crime accounts—that I am being shortchanged by my editor and my darling daughter, re: the number of chapters per volume I am allotted, there is no joy in Mudville (literary allusion) in my taking over the narrative from Brandy at this juncture.

You see, after the body of John Miller surfaced in the pond (and it was indeed John Miller, the fest's winner turned loser, who bobbed to the surface like a bar of Ivory soap) (metaphorical language is also something readers enjoy), the poor girl had to be conveyed by Tony back to the Pullman, where she with my blessing took one of my sleeping pills.

By the way, you wordsmiths may be jones-ing on my mastery of metaphor, wordplay, and literary allusion, but you need also remember to maintain a tight focus on the narrative that you are relating.

Where was I?

One would think that after all of the cases Brandy and I have solved (some of which proved fairly harrowing), the child might be accustomed to confronting the occasional corpse; in her defense, however, the bodies were piling up around Antiqua at a fairly alarming rate.

But, the show—which is to say, investigation—must go on, even in the wee small hours of a Sunday morning.

At the moment, the Serenity Search and Rescue team were out on the pond in rowboats with search lights, using drag bars with hooks to pinpoint the location of the late Mr. Miller, who had disappeared back down into the murky depths before Chief Cassato could snag him.

The bedraggled forensics team, Henderson and Wilson, were also hard at work, setting up a perimeter around the immediate area, along with a triage, although there would be no patient to whom administrating medical aid might serve helpful. Still, the coroner, once he arrived, would want the privacy for a preliminary evaluation of the remains.

The chief, upon returning from tucking Brandy in, joined me on the bank, near the boat dock.

I said, "*Death was in that poisonous wave, and in its gulf a fitting grave.*"

The chief's thick neck swiveled my way, eyes giving me an unblinking look. "Say what?"

"An Edgar Allan poem. 'The Lake.' "

He grunted.

I sighed. "I'm afraid we've underestimated our killer."

Another grunt.

"Although," I offered, "this could be a copycat mimicking the Poe allusions of the Crafton girl's murder and the attempted murder of the mayor."

Speaking of literary allusions, these crimes were rather extreme examples thereof.

"Why a copycat?" he asked, finally giving me more than a grunt.

"Someone who wanted the Poe book," I ventured, "might wish to confuse the issue by tying this death to the previous Poe-styled crimes. Paul Oldfield—who came in second place to the late Mr. Miller, where that valuable book is concerned—in particular comes to mind."

The chief was nodding. "This latest murder victim's motel room needs searching."

I had been just about to suggest that, but often great law enforcement minds think alike.

So I informed forensics of where Chief Cassato and I were heading, instructing them to notify me when Miller's body had been recovered.

With the chief's vehicle at city hall and mine still parked at the Pullman, we hoofed the short distance to the highway, where just within the city limits awaited the Tiki, a typical, small-town mom-and-pop motel that probably had seen its share of moms and pops over the years, since its Grand Opening Week guests might well have included Bonnie and Clyde.

The office was located in the center of the one-story structure, its NO VACANCY (inaccurate now) glowing, bookended on either side by four rooms, making a total of eight. An urn of geraniums greeted us outside the front door, and neon trim winked at us in pink and blue. We entered a small, brightly lit rustic room.

No one was behind the counter, so I hit a little bell, and shortly a curtain parted and out shuffled a tired-looking, stubble-faced, elderly gent in wire-frame glasses and a white shirt and bow tie (and presumably trousers of some kind, although the counter blocked that key information).

I suddenly reduced my estimation of the number of moms and pops in the Tiki Motel's history.

"Howdy, Sheriff," he addressed me.

"Ah! You recognize me. Did you perchance take in my performance of 'The Raven'?"

"No. I saw your badge. Just now."

"Oh. Nicely observed."

The chief was giving me a look for some reason. He could be such an enigma!

The elderly gent said, "What can I do you for?"

"This is my police consultant, Chief Cassato from Serenity. We'd like to see John Miller's room."

The old gent winced in thought, then reached for the phone on the counter. "Well, uh . . . not to stand on ceremony. But he could be in there now, and it might be more proper for me to give him a jingle first."

I raised my hand, smiled. "A jingle won't be necessary. What is your name, sir?"

"Rex J. Forsythe. I'm the owner."

"Well, Rex, if I may? I can assure you Mr. Miller is not in his room. Right now he's out at Antiqua park."

"What is he doing there?"

"Not much. Now, in the meantime, will you let us have a look at his room?"

He was frowning in confusion. "Isn't this the kind of thing that you should be showing me a warrant for?"

The chief said, "Why, Mr. Forsythe? Is there some reason we shouldn't see Mr. Miller's room?"

The owner shrugged. "Not that I can think of. It's just . . ."

The chief, starting to seem just a little impatient, said, "Just what, Mr. Forsythe?"

"Just . . ." the elderly gent said with a shrug. "This is the most excitement we ever had out at the Tiki. Except maybe for things that go on behind closed doors."

I beamed at him. "Isn't that always the case? Shall we?"

The chief and I followed the owner to number six, where our host unlocked the door with his passkey.

"Thank you, sir," I said. "That will be all."

The old boy hesitated, eyes blinking behind the wire-framed lenses. "You're not expecting any gunfire or the like?"

The chief said, "Probably not."

"Well . . . okay then," the owner said, and scurried back to the office. Scurry being a relative term, considering his age.

I opened the door, entered, flicked on the lights, slowly scanned the room, and then gasped. "Good Lord!"

The chief, reacting behind me, asked, "What *is* it, Vivian?"

Barely able to maintain my composure, I said, "Over there!"

His hand hovered reflexively over his right side, where he normally would have carried his weapon. He took a few steps past me. "*Where?*"

"On the wall, above the bed!"

He narrowed his eyes, shook his head. "I don't see what you're—"

"The *painting!*" I said. "Check the lower right corner!" The man might be a first-rate police officer, but he could be so thick sometimes. I could see it from *here!*

The chief walked over to the framed portrait of a pretty island girl, painted on black velvet, and leaned in. "All I see is 'Edgar Leeteg, Tahiti.'"

"Exactly! Leeteg is the father of black velvet paintings. He started the trend when living in Tahiti after Double-you Double-you Two. Some of his works can go for tens of thousands of dollars, and that ain't coconuts! What a find!"

The chief, apparently unimpressed, was covering his face with a hand.

"If that painting were missing," I said, "we'd have our murder motive!"

"But it's not missing," he said quietly.

My eyes flew to the pair of lamps on either side of the bed. "Good Lord! And those appear to be vintage *chalkware*. Continental Art Company, unless I miss my bet! You don't know how rare it is to find *both* the male and female figures . . . although they appear more *Hawaiian* in their garb than Tahitian."

"Vivian . . ."

Rotating, I gasped yet again. "And will you *look* at all this original Heywood-Wakefield furniture! I've never seen a complete bedroom set in the bamboo style before. Headboard, dresser, two end tables . . . very rare, indeed. And there's even a bamboo chair with floral cushion! Granted, the wood varnish has seen better days, and some of the bamboo is missing, but nothing that couldn't be restored."

I had run out of breath. The chief was just looking at me. I said, "What?"

He looked rather flushed.

"Don't you feel well?" I asked.

"This is a possible crime scene," he reminded me through clenched teeth. "It's not a yard sale."

"Oh, treasures like these just never turn up at yard sales. Well, perhaps *occasionally* . . ."

He took the Lord's name in vain rather loudly, making me jump.

Poor man must be tired. I mean, he'd had a heck of a night. I, myself, had felt fatigued just moments ago, but all these motel room goodies had given me a welcome jolt of adrenaline.

"We should probably get to work," I advised him. He'd dillydallied enough.

I unzipped a pouch on my duty belt and produced two

pairs of latex gloves, which we put on. The chief, looking strangely glazed, moved to the bathroom while I stayed put.

The bed was still made, though indications were that Miller had been in the room since its last cleaning: an ashtray brimmed with butts on one of two nightstands, and a used towel lay crumpled on the floor.

There was no closet, so I walked over to the dresser—noting a few deep scratches on the top, which would lower its value—and opened each of three drawers, finding them empty. Apparently their contents had been transferred to a duffle bag, open on the floor, indicating that Miller had not planned on staying the night, little suspecting he would be checking out even earlier, and from more than just this motel room.

Crossing over to the nearest nightstand—cigarette burns on the surface could make refinishing difficult—I opened its single drawer, discovering only a Gideons Bible.

I rounded the bed to the other nightstand, where I found its drawer empty.

From the doorway of the bathroom, the chief asked, "Anything, Vivian?"

"The lamp's female figure has a large crack," I said, "and it could be restored, but matching the color would be tricky."

"I mean anything pertinent to our investigation."

"Not yet. Still looking!"

Then I spotted a business card for Relics Antiques at my feet and picked it up with latex-protected fingers. Not easy to do! A handwritten phone number on the back of the card differed from the one on the front.

Tony approached. "Something?"

I showed him the card.

"Looks like Paula gave Mr. Miller her *personal* number," I said. "Might be interesting to learn why."

"Might at that. Anything else?"

"No. You?"

He shrugged. "The usual toiletries . . . but there is some chalky powder on the floor, which forensics should have a look at. Might be talcum. Might be something else."

I nodded. "I take it the late occupant didn't use Poe's expensive *Tales* as bathroom reading."

"Not hardly."

"And the book isn't out here anywhere. Mr. Miller must have taken it with him." I shrugged. "Perhaps someone offered to buy it."

He was nodding. "And they met, probably at the park, for a quiet transaction."

"And, instead of transacting, the 'buyer' dispatched the 'seller' forthwith."

"Seems the best explanation," the chief said. "I certainly see no evidence that the man was killed here."

"Nor do I."

The chief sighed. "I'm heading back to Serenity. I can do more good for us there than here. Want to hit the PD computer and find out more about John Miller and Paul Oldfield."

I said, "Would be nice to know Oldfield's movements after I told him to get out of Dodge. He should have long since returned to Illinois."

"I can follow up on that. Tell Brandy I'll check in with her later, would you?"

I nodded. "I'll wait here for forensics."

He headed out, leaving the door open.

My cell sang its Hawaiian song in keeping with the Leeteg and the lamps.

Forensics tech Henderson was calling to say the rescue team had just pulled Miller's body from the pond. I told him he and his partner, Wilson, needed to come over to the Tiki to process Miller's room when they were finished at the park. His response betrayed a lack of enthusiasm for further wee-hours work. What exactly he said is something I shan't repeat here.

I made myself as comfortable as I could in the Heywood-Wakefield bamboo chair, knowing they would be a while.

I was thinking about how difficult and convoluted these particular murders were when I had a sudden revelation! Sometimes all the puzzle pieces suddenly fit, all the tumblers on the lock click, and the world opens up like a clamshell!

I couldn't believe it hadn't occurred to me earlier!

Maybe the other rooms in this motel contained the same vintage furnishings as this one! I could cherry-pick the best pieces, the nicest chalkware lamps, but do my darndest to snag every single one of the Edgar Leeteg black velvet paintings!

I settled farther into the chair, resting my head against the bamboo back. Maybe something about the case itself would occur to me.

Should I tell Mr. Forsthye of the value of his furnishings? Or let "seller beware?" I *could* be truthful about the furniture—pointing out the costly restoration—and lowball the paintings, as the market for Leeteg *had* softened in recent years . . . or, I could be truthful about the paintings, and lowball the furniture.

I yawned. Of course, I was assuming that the elderly owner had little knowledge of the antiques among us, which could make negotiation brutal, just murder. . . .

Then everything went black!

Had I been struck a blow from behind? Would I be dragged to a crypt and stuffed into a sarcophagus like poor Morella, to suffer a premature burial?

Sorry to disappoint you, dear reader, but I merely fell asleep, dreaming of Tahiti and bamboo furniture.

* * *

Brandy back.

Apologies. That one hurt a little, didn't it?

Anyway, after the peal of a church bell woke me, it took a moment before I realized I was in bed in the Pullman. I looked at my cell phone on the nightstand: 9:45 a.m. I climbed out from under the covers, somewhat groggy from the sleeping pill, and went over to part the window curtains.

Outside, the sun was shining, the lack of moisture on the glass indicating a cooler temperature. Looked like a nice day for a change.

But not for John Miller.

I pushed any thought of my ghastly discovery of him out of my mind, and I wandered out of the bedroom, looking for Mother. Not finding her, I returned to get my cell phone and call her. I got her on a single ring.

Mother, sounding remarkably chipper, said she was still tied up with forensics and that Tony had returned to Serenity to do some investigating on that end and would call me later.

"Would you like to be helpful, dear?"

"Sure," I lied.

"Why don't you go to this morning's service?" She'd heard that bell too. "Might be just the thing to make you feel better. You could send up a prayer for that poor soul in the pond. Well, he's out of the pond now, but you know what I mean."

Church did sound better than joining her at a crime scene, and there was nothing to do in the Pullman but sleep some more, which just seemed sad.

I said, "Church is fine."

"Yes, good for the soul! And for studying suspects."

Right then something I'd meant to mention to her popped into my head.

"Mother, Saturday morning I was in Paula's store when John Miller came in."

"Oh? Really? Interesting! What was her reaction?"

"She looked surprised to see him, and kind of upset. She pretended not to know him, but it seemed obvious she did. And I'm sure he was there on some kind of pretense. Then they went off to talk where I couldn't hear them."

She said, "Interesting" again but didn't explain.

I wasn't in a frame of mind to ask why, either. So we signed off, thankfully minus any police codes.

Sushi, who'd finally roused from slumber, was asking to go out, and after I'd done my dog-owner duty, I took a quick shower and found something clean to wear. It now was a quarter after ten.

When I arrived at the church, the doors were closed and singing could be heard from within.

I slipped inside, spotted a place at the end of the back row, just as the hymn "Nearer, My God, To Thee" ended, and everyone sat down.

I was surprised by how many people were there, after Pastor Creed's lament about dwindling membership. Maybe some tourists were present. Anyway, considering the trying events of the past few days, I figured folks needed some spiritual comforting.

Rubbernecking a bit, I noticed the council members were in attendance, scattered throughout the congregation: Wally and a woman I took to be wife Stella, Paula with Lottie, and Rick near the back. Mayor Hatcher and his wife, Caroline, were positioned rather conspicuously in the first pew.

Pastor Creed, poised at the pulpit, opened his Bible and gazed out over his somewhat shell-shocked flock.

"Recently our small community has been faced with tragedy and strife. How can one cope? By giving comfort to one another, helping one another, and sharing the pain and sorrow. And, most important, by praying with all your heart from the depth of your soul. Please join me in the Lord's Prayer." He bowed his head. "Our Father who art in Heaven . . ."

The congregation spoke as one.

That show of unity was kind of nice, yet I couldn't help but wonder if this represented all the consideration poor Morella was likely to receive. Or the lucky-to-still-be-alive Myron. Not to mention that outsider, John Miller. . . .

When the Lord's Prayer had concluded, Creed intoned, "Our scripture for today is taken from Deuteronomy 19:15."

The woman beside me whispered to her husband, "That's not what's in the program."

"One witness shall not rise up against a man for any iniquity, or for any sin, in any sin that he sinneth: at the mouth of two witnesses, or at the mouth of three witnesses, shall the matter be established." The pastor closed the Bible. "What God is telling us through Moses is that laws are . . ."

That was when I stopped listening, my brain flatlining while I stared at the man's bad toupee in front of me. If God in all His glory had removed this guy's hair, how could a mere mortal hope to get away with a rug like that?

Another hymn brought me to my feet—"How Great Thou Art"—after which the choir sang something modern, and they sounded pretty good. Afterward, everyone settled in for the sermon.

Pastor Creed spoke in a firm baritone that gave his words weight. "The Bible teaches us that at the final judgment, the righteous will enter Heaven and have everlasting life, but the wicked will go to Hell and have eternal punishment. We know what Heaven is. But what is Hell?" He paused for effect. "Hell is a place of darkness and fire with no rest or relief. . . ."

Okay. This was not my idea of finding comfort, so I zoned out again.

After what seemed like an eternity of punishment doled out right here on earth, the sermon concluded, and everybody stretched their legs for the final hymn, "What a Friend We Have in Jesus."

After the first stanza, I slipped out to avoid talking to anyone—especially council members who might have noticed or heard about the activity at the park late last night.

Back at the Pullman, Mother was in the parlor, on her knees as if for a Sunday morning prayer.

No such luck.

She was, instead, crouched before the big borrowed chalkboard, which was propped up against the couch. I could tell by her expression she was having trouble compiling her suspect list, which looked like this:

Suspects:	MORELLA motive/opp.	MAYOR HATCHER motive/opp.	JOHN MILLER motive/opp.
Paula Baxter	?/yes	?/yes	?/?
Lottie Everhart	?/yes	?/yes	?/?
Wally Thorp	argument/?	?/yes	?/?
Rick Wheeler	?/yes	?/yes	?/?
Myron Hatcher	affair/no	Not applicable	?/?
Pastor Creed	angry/yes	angry/yes	?/?
Paul Oldfield	?/?	?/?	Poe book/yes

She looked over her shoulder at me. "It's a work in progress, dear. Unfortunately, I'm not making any."

"That's a lot of question marks," I pointed out.

"Also a lot of opportunity."

"There could be *two* killers, you know."

"I'm aware of that! Sorry . . . didn't mean to snap. How was church? Anyone ask about last night?" She raised a hand for assistance in getting up, which I provided.

"I avoided talking to anyone," I said. "What happened after I took that sedative last night?"

Standing now, Mother filled me in: The coroner's initial opinion was that Miller had been struck a blow on the head before being dumped into the pond, where he drowned. She also detailed her search of Miller's hotel room with Tony. I forbade her from elaborating on the kitschy motel room finds.

I asked, "What do you think happened to the book?"

She was studying the chalkboard. "Whoever killed Miller has it, most certainly."

My eyes went to the board as well. "Paul Oldfield is the only one with both motive and opportunity."

"I have no argument with that analysis."

My cell phone rang. Tony.

"How are you doing?" he asked.

"Okay. That pill really put me out. No dreams that I remember."

"Good." His tone turned business-like. "Is Vivian handy?"

Vaguely annoyed that Tony just dumped me for Mother, I handed her my cell but stayed close enough to hear both ends of the conversation.

"Yes, Chief?"

"I checked on Paul Oldfield. He *did* leave town yesterday afternoon. Made it back to Morris, Illinois, by early evening. He and his wife entertained. Their guests stayed late. No way he could have made it back to Antiqua."

Mother's face soured. "I see."

"But I do have some interesting information on John Miller, and 'interesting' understates it. His real name is Owen Phillips. Twenty-some years ago he served time for armed robbery in Indiana."

"Well! Some antiques dealer!"

"Actually, he *is* in the antiques business. He's even connected to someone in that trade in Antiqua. Seems there was an accomplice who went to prison as well. I'm sending both mug shots to your e-mail."

While I kept the line open on my phone, Mother's cell beeped, and she reached for it. In a few seconds she had opened the attachment.

I looked over her shoulder. The first photo was a younger version of Miller, aka Phillips.

The second one sent our mouths dropping and our eyes popping.

The photo was of a much younger Paula Baxter, a mug shot with her holding a placard reading BETTY RITTER.

Mother spoke into the cell again. "Chief, what else can you tell me about Paula, or should I say, Betty?"

"Nothing, really. Seems to have stayed clean. Made a fresh start, a new life for herself there in Antiqua."

"And then," Mother said, melodramatically, "along comes someone out of her past."

"Yes," replied Tony.

"I'll go interview her now," Mother said. "When are you coming back?"

"I want to check in with forensics first. See if they've found out what that substance in the motel room is."

"Drugs, you think? That 'talcum,' maybe?"

"Let you know."

His end went silent.

I said, "That explains why Paula seemed so surprised, shocked even, when John Miller turned up on her doorstep."

Mother nodded. "It does indeed. Shall we avail her of an opportunity to explain herself?"

At around one in the afternoon, we went in an unlocked door at the rear of Paula's building, finding a narrow stairwell up to her apartment. From behind the closed door on the landing came the sound of a television turned up loud enough to hear the banter between two baseball announcers.

With no doorbell to ring, Mother knocked with considerable force.

The TV volume decreased and, after a few moments, the door opened.

Paula, casually attired in an oversized yellow T-shirt and blue jean capris, her feet bare, said, "Oh . . . Sheriff! I'm glad you're here."

Very likely she would soon come to regret those words.

"Do come in." Paula stepped aside, we entered, and she shut the door.

The living room, a good size, had a beige carpet, white walls, and modern furnishings. No antiques seemed to have followed her home.

Regarding the decor, Paula said, "I spend all day with fun old stuff, but I am not about to do that at night. Please, have a seat."

She shooed a tabby cat off the floral couch. "Can I get either of you something cold to drink?"

Mother declined on our behalf, and we settled onto the sofa.

Paula crossed to an overstuffed chair, sat, then said, "There are rumors going around about a drowning at the pond late last night. Are they true?"

"They are," Mother said.

"Someone I . . . know?"

"Someone you know."

"Oh, dear. *Who?*"

"John Miller."

Paula's eyes widened, and her mouth yawned open.

After a few speechless moments, she said, "Isn't that the, uh, winner? The man who found the valuable book?"

"Yes."

"It was a drowning? In the park? An accident? Could you be a little more . . . forthcoming?"

"I believe it was murder," Mother told her. "Although we won't know for a certainty until after the autopsy."

Paula was shaking her head. "I just *knew* there would be trouble over that book."

Mother smiled. "Certainly whoever is behind these bizarre murders would like us to think so."

Paula stared at her. "What other reason could there be?"

Mother's smile just went on and on. "I thought perhaps *you* might have a theory about that. Which you might care to share."

Paula's eyebrows climbed. "Why *would* I?"

"Well, you *knew* him, didn't you, dear?"

She was shaking her mop of red hair as she said, "Sheriff, I only met him the other day, when he came into my store." She looked at me. "*You* were there! Did it look like we knew each other?"

"Kind of," I said with a shrug.

Mother's fingers had been busy on her cell, loading the dual mug shots on the screen. "Perhaps you knew him under a different name—a rose by any name being as sweet." She held up the phone. "Owen Phillips?"

Paula paled.

"And perhaps you may remember *this* person. . . ." The second mug shot filled the screen. "Betty Ritter."

Paula didn't bother looking, just stared blankly at the TV, where a batter was striking out.

"It would save all of us a terrible amount of trouble," Mother said, "yourself included, if you would just admit what you did. Was it a struggle that got out of hand, an accident really? And you dumped your former partner-in-crime's unconscious body in the lake? Maybe you thought he was *already* dead . . ."

This finally rocked the woman out of her silence. "I didn't *kill* Owen! Yes, okay, I admit he and I shared a past—but we served our sentences and went our separate ways. Lived our own, very separate lives."

I asked, "Did you know he'd gone into the antiquing business too?"

Her eyes went to mine. "Yes. It was always a shared interest. And"—she shrugged—"I had kept track of him a little . . . knew he had a store in Indiana, and changed his name to John Miller." She paused. "But two days ago was the first time I'd seen, or heard from, him in years." She paused. "Can't you see? I've built myself a new life, a new reputation."

She'd also built herself a genuine motive for murder.

Mother asked, "Where were you last night?"

The words came out in a rush. "I came here after the meeting, fixed myself some dinner, watched a movie on cable. Then I took a sleeping pill, as is my habit, and went to bed. And no, I don't have anyone who could back that up."

I asked, "What did John—Owen—want when he came to your store? And I don't buy for a second that he was looking for a candlestick phone."

Paula sighed. "My assumption was he wanted money for his silence. So I let him know I had very little cash, if he had any intention of trying to blackmail me."

Mother asked, "*Was* that his intention?"

Paula sighed. "Of sorts."

"Explain."

"He said he wanted to use my business in some way or other."

Mother frowned. "Was he looking to form a partnership?"

Paula shrugged. "He couldn't say, because I had customers. He wanted my cell number, so I gave it to him. And he said we'd talk later."

"And did you?"

She shook her head. "I never found out what he had in mind. But if I knew him, and I did, whatever it was wasn't likely to be strictly legit."

Could be for smuggling drugs, I thought, remembering that white powder Mother mentioned. Or using a legit antiques shop to fence stolen or faked pieces.

Mother asked, "How do you think he found you?"

"I can't say. I've stayed off social media, and don't even have my picture on my web page."

Mother moved on. "Who else knew about your past? Any of the council members?"

"Myron did," Paula said.

"How did he come to know?"

She shrugged. "I told him. Before I ran for the council. I trusted Myron, and wanted him to know about my past— that I'd had this relationship with Owen Phillips, who'd changed his name to John Miller, and was an antiques dealer. And that my name used to be Betty Ritter."

Mother nodded. "And what did Myron say?"

"He said I'd paid for my crime, that I was a good citizen, and my business was a boon to the town. He thought I'd make a great addition to the council and saw no reason to dredge up the past. He was very decent about it."

I asked, "He never held it over you?"

Paula's eyes flashed. "If you're referring to blackmail, no."

"There are forms of pressure other than demanding cash," I said. "Your vote on the council, for instance."

"I resent that," Paula snapped. "Myron has never pressured me for my vote on anything."

"But," I pressed, "you might feel an obligation."

Paula thought about that. "Perhaps. But that hasn't happened yet."

Mother rose, saying, "I believe that's all for now. I'll have to ask you not to leave town."

"Of course," she said, also standing, as was I. "Can you keep what you've learned to yourselves?"

Mother said, "As long as making it known isn't necessary to bringing a killer to justice."

She swallowed. "Thank you."

We left.

Outside, Mother faced me. "Well?"

"I tend to believe her."

Mother seemed annoyed by my answer. "She has a good motive for killing Miller, and no alibi. It's only her word that she was at home."

The church bell began to ring.

Mother looked in that direction. "*Hear the tolling of the bells—Iron bells!*" she proclaimed. "*What a world of solemn thought their monody compels.*"

"Why is it ringing now? This is Sunday afternoon, not morning."

Abruptly, her expression changed. "Is there some special church service this afternoon? A memorial for Morella, perhaps?"

"Not that I know of."

The ringing became erratic.

I sucked in air. "Mother . . . !"

Though we were on the run, heading toward the church,

it felt as though we were moving in slow motion, time stretching out interminably, until finally we reached it.

The bell had gone silent.

Mother, out of breath, stood before the door. "Stay out here, dear."

"No! I'm going in," I said, mad at myself for my prior squeamishness.

I pushed past her, rushed in, and ran straight into Pastor Creed.

Who was hanging from the rope of the bell.

A Trash 'n' Treasures Tip

Many top booksellers print high-quality color-picture catalogs of their stock, showcasing their best inventory. Requesting these beautiful catalogs is an easy way to get (and keep on hand) accurate information on collectible and rare books. I threw out a stack of these one time, and Mother didn't speak to me for days. Wasn't bad!

Chapter Ten

Faux Poe

I grabbed onto Pastor Creed's dangling legs and, best as I could, hoisted him up to ease, I hoped, the pressure from the rope cutting into his neck.

At the same time, I yelled to Mother, "Help me get him down!"

The pastor couldn't have been hanging for very long, the erratic ringing of the bell having indicated a struggle stopping only minutes ago.

Mother found a chair, dragged it over, and climbed onto its seat, then withdrew the Swiss army knife from her duty belt. This allowed her to reach above the pastor's head, even with me holding him up some. Stretching, she began sawing away at the somewhat slackened rope.

This took a while, and I was straining with the weight, but she stayed at it and so did I. When seemingly endless minutes finally did end, the rope snapped and now the pastor's full poundage dropped. I collapsed as Creed came tumbling down on top of me.

"Mother!" I cried. Whether I was summoning the sheriff or nearly swearing in church, who can say?

"Coming, dear," she said, and did, rolling the possible corpse off me. He lay facedown on the floor, the top half of him extending into the central aisle.

Mother rolled the pastor onto his back and began vigorous chest compressions while singing the Bee Gees' disco hit "Stayin' Alive," pushing to the song's fast beat. Every so often she'd blow into his mouth, at first having some trouble getting the man's tongue out of the way.

She kept this up for a good minute, then gestured for me to take over. Pretty well recovered from my earlier efforts, including having a grown man fall on me, I followed her lead (opting not to sing) while she got out her cell phone.

"Ben!" She barked. "Sheriff Borne."

Ben? I thought. *Ben who?*

She was saying, "Does the reservation have paramedics?"

Ah! Ben Saukenuk, the Tomahawk casino manager Mother had met on her investigative travels.

"Good," she said. "I need them to come to the church in Antiqua ASAP. There's been an apparent suicide attempt, a hanging, and the individual might still be revived. And you're the closest help. Can you put that in motion? Good. Thank you!"

I wondered how long someone's brain could be deprived of oxygen before permanent damage set in. Was there a point at which it might be better to stop trying?

Mother took back over. On her next compression, Creed made a gurgling sound.

"He's *breathing!*" she exclaimed, pleased with her work.

The pastor's chest moved ever so slightly up and down, but his face remained placid, eyes closed, no movement behind the lids.

Mother sat back. "Nothing to do now but wait."

But I didn't want to stand there, or kneel there actually, even if this *was* a house of worship. So I got to my feet and walked toward the sanctuary. Off to one side was the door to the pastor's office.

I went in.

In the center of his desk, perfectly arranged, was a computer-typed letter, a single sheet. I leaned in to read it, careful not to touch the paper.

I killed Morella Crafton, John Miller, and tried to kill Myron Hatcher.

May the Lord God forgive me.

No signature.

"Hmmm," I said.

That was interesting. But perhaps not as interesting as the book next to it, also neatly arranged: *Tales* by Edgar Allan Poe. And not just any edition: the one that many visitors to Antiqua had rushed around town looking for, and that two men fought over in the street, one of whom died not long after, with the rare book—*this* rare book—conspicuously absent from his possession.

I returned to Mother, still on the floor seated next to the prone, breathing, but unconscious Creed.

"Some items worth seeing on the pastor's desk," I told her. "I'll stay with him while you go have a look."

With the help of my hand, she got to her feet, and I took her place by Creed, ready to resume CPR if need be.

After a few minutes Mother returned, wearing a gleeful expression, which was unsettling considering the circumstances.

"My theory," she said, beaming, "of Creed being our killer is now confirmed."

I looked up at her. "Is it?"

"Of course it is, dear." She started ticking off on her fingers. "*One*, he was upset about the continued illicit use of the mausoleum and summoned Morella there by calling her from city hall, using the key he was given but never returned. *Two*, miffed with the mayor over the mausoleum and this distasteful festival, he attacked Myron, walling him up in the church basement. And, *three*, he drowned Miller, who had possession of the Poe book, knowing that would put a stop to the dreaded festival. But finally everything caught up with him, and *four*, distressed by what he had done, he hanged himself. It all fits, very neatly."

"Maybe too neatly?"

She blinked at me, her lenses magnifying the response. "Your point being?"

"Well, we could start with that suicide letter—unsigned."

"Many such tragic missives go unsigned, dear. People driven to the point of self-destruction seldom do as one might expect."

"Also, it's not handwritten."

"Why bother with formalities at such a time?"

"What more formal a time is there than pausing before taking your life to tell the world why? An unsigned, typewritten suicide note, Mother? What if this were a *Perry Mason* rerun? Or an Agatha Christie novel?"

"First, *Perry Mason* is nothing *but* reruns. Second, this is *real* life, not some ridiculous novel. Meaning no offense to Dame Agatha."

"And isn't it nicely convenient to find the book right there with the letter?" I paused. "Would Pastor Creed, feeling as he did about Poe's work, even bring such a volume into his church? He would more likely *burn* it."

The sheriff's stare morphed into a glare.

Creed, eyes closed, had no opinion to share at the moment.

Mother stomped her foot. "Damnit!" Her eyes went briefly to the ceiling. "Forgive me." Then, reluctantly, she admitted quietly, "You're right. The pastor also appears to have been hit on the back of his head, the same M.O. as the other victims. I now believe this fine, if rather misguided, man of the cloth was framed. It's a good thing I took the time to think this through."

"Isn't it?" I said.

A siren called in the distance.

"I want to check the parsonage," I said. "Give me some of those latex gloves from your Bat belt."

She did.

I left the church and made my way briskly along a worn path leading to a nearby stone cottage, perhaps built around the same time as the mausoleum and sheltered by several tall oaks. I was not surprised to find the heavy wooden door unlocked.

The interior was clean, modest, but comfortable—lots of dark wood, a mix of modern and midcentury including probable antiques and collectibles that no doubt would have distracted Mother. The front room had a worn hardwood floor with area rugs and a stone fireplace with a small dining table and four chairs, also a couch and end tables and two easy chairs. To the left was a galley kitchen, and to the right a short hallway that led to the bathroom and bedroom.

From the bedroom window I could see the back and right side of the church, which included most of the parking lot, where a boxy white ambulance was now parked. On the windowsill were binoculars, and I picked them up to have a closer look.

The double doors of the ambulance, which had SAUK NATION EMERGENCY MEDICAL CARE in blue on its side, were opened wide as two men removed a retractable gurney.

Then it hit me.

Pastor Creed claimed that because of the leafy fullness of the trees, he hadn't been able to see anyone entering the church basement the night of Mayor Hatcher's abduction. But in reality, the branches were well up and out of the way.

And wasn't that the purpose of the binoculars? To clearly monitor any unwanted activity going on around the church?

What had Pastor Creed seen Friday night?

Had he been wakened in the early morning hours by the headlights of a car as it pulled into the church parking lot? Drawn to the window, had he picked up the binoculars and witnessed one or two people get out of the vehicle, then carry a third person to the basement's wooden storm cellar doors?

This seemed likely and, if so, he must have recognized that individual or individuals. But why would he keep silent about it? That didn't seem to make sense.

I retraced my steps to the front room and went over to an old upright writing desk. From the pigeon holes, I pulled out various papers and examined them; they were mostly bills and church correspondence, nothing of any apparent significance.

The center main drawer contained stationery, envelopes, pens, stamps, and so forth. The top drawer to the left held Creed's personal bank account statements, with modest balances; the bottom one stored files on various topics for sermons. The top right drawer had paid receipts; the one below was a catch-all, where finally I did find something of interest: *an architect's rendering of a new church, and parsonage!*

For all his humbleness, Pastor Creed seemed not to have been content to live as modestly as he had been.

I returned the drawing to the drawer and left the stone cottage to return to the church.

In the parking lot, two Sauk paramedics—men attired in navy blue slacks and shirts with tribal insignia on the sleeves—loaded the gurney with the unconscious, oxygen-masked Creed into their vehicle.

Mother was positioned nearby, talking on her cell.

"Thank you, Ben," she was saying. "I've instructed them to take the pastor to the hospital in Serenity. . . . Yes, I know, and please tell the tribal council I'll be happy to make a case for my actions at a later time, and we can talk about remuneration. Also, please convey how extremely grateful I am."

She exchanged good-byes with the casino manager, then returned her cell to her pocket.

"Have you been in contact with Tony?" I asked.

Mother nodded. "He'll be providing twenty-four-seven security for Creed at the hospital."

"And forensics?"

She sighed. "Unhappy campers. Perhaps they *should* just take a room at the Tiki Motel."

We watched the white van pull away, the wail of its siren a modern war cry.

About a dozen folks had been drawn out of their homes by the activity, though thus far they were watching from a respectful distance.

Mother, eyeing them as if a zombie horde were waiting to launch a shambling attack, said, "Let us move inside, dear."

We did, closing the door, then moving to a rear pew.

Once seated, angled toward each other, Mother asked, "What did you find?"

I told her about the unobstructed view of the church from the bedroom, the binoculars, and the discovery of plans for building a new church . . . and parsonage.

Mother consumed that, saying nothing.

I asked, "Anything from Tony?"

She nodded. "He said the coroner reported that John Miller, that is, Owen Phillips—"

I interrupted. "Can we just agree to call him Miller? I don't have a program to refer to, you know."

"As you like. Where was I?"

"The coroner reported that . . ."

"That Miller had been hit on the head, but whether that was a killing blow, we won't know until after the autopsy."

I nodded. "If there's water in his lungs, that will tell the story."

"Also, the powder found in the motel room? Is a mixture of lime, sand, and cement."

"Mortar!" I exclaimed, not taking time to chide her for uptalking.

"The precise recipe."

"Which means Miller was involved in the attack on the mayor." I frowned. "But Miller was already dead when somebody hanged Creed and faked the suicide."

She nodded. "Seems an accomplice was going around trying to tie off loose ends."

"Yes," I said, "with a rope!"

We sat quietly, the careening events stunning both of us, I think. But sitting there in the church made me recall something.

"Mother, Pastor Creed's scripture reading this morning—it differed from what was listed in the bulletin."

She frowned a little. "Do you find that significant?"

"Maybe. I mean, since the program was probably printed days ago, what made Creed change his mind?"

Now she was nodding, just barely. "What *was* the scripture, dear?"

"Well, I don't know exactly. I'm no Bible scholar. But I think he said from the pulpit that he was reading from Deuteronomy."

"Deuteronomy concerns the law in Moses's day," Mother said, nodding again, with somewhat more force. "Could you be more specific?"

"Something about witnesses?"

Excitement came into her eyes and her voice: "Could it

have been Deuteronomy 19:15? To paraphrase, one witness to a crime is not sufficient to convict, but two or more
could?"

"That's it!" But then I was only more confused. "What
two witnesses could he have been talking about? Witnesses
to what?"

Mother smiled cagily. "Not *witnesses*, dear. The point
of the scripture is that there was only one witness. And to
one of these crimes."

"The pastor?"

"The pastor. Now, this is important—who among the
council members attended the service?"

"All of them."

"You're sure?"

"Positive."

Mother turned away from me, her eyes on the cross. "So
whose ears, do you suppose, were the last-minute scripture
lesson intended for?"

Her cell phone blasted the *Hawaii Five-O* theme.

Myron Hatcher's voice was loud enough for me to hear.
"Sheriff! I received a call about seeing an ambulance from
the Indian reservation at the church. What's *that* about?"

"That is not information I can share over the phone,
Mayor. But would you assemble the council at city hall,
say . . . in half an hour? I'd rather explain to everyone at
the same time."

"Is Pastor Creed all right? The caller said ambulance at-
tendants were—"

"Half an hour. Thank you."

She clicked off and pocketed the cell.

A new forensics unit arrived—a man and women borrowed from Burlington, a city just south of Serenity, the
team from Serenity having been overworked. After brief
introductions, Mother filled the pair in, instructing them to

pay particular attention to the evidence found in the pastor's office. An examination of the parsonage would come later.

Mother gave the new techs her cell number, then she and I left them to their work.

The downtown was nearly deserted as we made our way on foot to city hall. Festival activities had been scheduled for Sunday afternoon, including a screening of Vincent Price in *House of Usher* at a nearby consolidated high school auditorium, and stores had planned on being open as well. But in the wake of this series of tragedies, only the coffee shop was business as usual.

When Mother and I entered the conference room, we found the council members seated in their churchgoing attire, looking beleaguered and demoralized. Not arranged in a straight line this time, they were seated on either side of the table, leaving spaces between them. Perhaps no one cared to be seated next to a possible killer.

With no greeting, Mother took a position with her back to the wall where the chalkboard used to be. I stood off to one side.

"About an hour ago," Mother said, "I, along with my deputy, discovered Pastor Creed inside the church—hanging from the bell cord."

Even though word of the man being taken away by ambulance had circulated, this news brought gasps. Eyes were wide all around, heads shaking.

Mother raised a silencing palm. "In the pastor's office was a suicide letter. Also, the antique Edgar Allan Poe book, which had last been in the possession of the late John Miller."

Lottie raised a hand, as if in class. "Was he the person who drowned in the pond last night?"

"Yes. Or perhaps we should say *was* drowned."

Murmurs.

Rick didn't bothering raising his hand. "What did this suicide note say?"

"It was a confession," Mother said. "To killing Morella Crafton and John Miller, and of the attempted murder of Mayor Myron Hatcher."

The revelation brought His Honor to his feet. "I don't believe that for a second! Pastor Creed would *never* have done any of those things. He was the heart of Antiqua's spiritual life!"

I noticed Mother was not correcting the false impression that the pastor had died.

Paula said, "Myron, have you forgotten Pastor Creed's deep dislike of the festival honoring Poe—and he wasn't exactly shy of expressing his displeasure with your role in it either."

Rick snorted. "Remember how Creed blew a gasket over that mausoleum not being repaired?"

Myron almost collapsed back into his chair, all the air let out of him.

Lottie sighed. "Then the pastor murdered this Miller person, just because the man won that *book?* Isn't that a little difficult to believe?"

Paula seemed puzzled. "And what would Pastor Creed have had against Morella?"

The council members all turned their faces toward Mother for enlightenment. Me, I was watching Wally, whose expression was strained, jaw clenched.

Mother admitted, "I don't have an answer to any of that."

There was silence.

Then Myron said quietly, "I might."

Now all eyes went to him. Including mine.

"About a month ago," the mayor began, "I dropped by the church to speak to Creed about the fund-raising for the basement construction. When I didn't find him in his office, I walked over to the parsonage." He paused. "Well, he let me in, and as we went over the donations I'd received so far, I noticed a particular scent in the room . . . which I recognized as the perfume Morella wore."

I think my expression upon hearing that prompted the mayor to amend his comments.

He said, "I think anyone who ever had that young woman wait on them at the coffee shop would back me up—it was quite a strong fragrance, you know, and very distinctive."

Some nodding of heads.

"Anyway," Myron went on, "I left, and returned to my car in the parking lot, and I was about to leave when Morella came out of the parsonage."

You could see the wheels in Wally's head turning—you could almost hear them. His daughter hadn't been involved with a married man, after all—but the *pastor!*

"So what?" Rick said with a shrug. "Creed wasn't a priest. He was allowed a private life."

"That's true," Lottie said, "but why hide the affair?"

"There must be more to it than that," Paula suggested, perhaps a little too eagerly.

"Stop it!" Myron said. "Now I'm sorry I even *mentioned* it. Isn't there enough rumormongering going on? We may never know the 'why' of it, with both parties dead."

"Oh," Mother said, "but Pastor Creed is not dead."

No gasps this time—just jaws dropping.

"But," Lottie said, "you *told* us he was!"

"No, dear. I said he was hanged. My deputy and I managed to revive him."

I was almost starting to like the sound of that.

"Thank the Lord," Myron said softly.

Rick asked, "Has Creed said anything?"

"Unfortunately, no," Mother replied. "At least not yet. He's unconscious. But he's getting the best of care at the hospital in Serenity."

Personally, I would have withheld Creed's whereabouts, waiting to see who would ask first. But I was only the deputy.

Lottie sighed. "Well, at least the madman has been caught, however unlikely his identity might seem to us."

"Perhaps not," Mother said.

Lottie blinked. "It's *not* unlikely?"

"The pastor may not be the 'madman.' He may just be the latest victim."

Frowning, Rick asked, "What do you mean?"

"There's another possible explanation for the hanging—a rather more complicated one. Even complex."

Mother paused, milking the moment; you can take the diva out of the theater, but you can't take the theater out of the diva.

She continued: "Suppose the pastor was hit on the back of his head—as was the case with Morella, Myron, and Miller—and then hanged, making it *look* like suicide."

Rick asked, "*Was* he?"

"Was he what, dear?"

"Hit on the back of his head!" the young man echoed irritably.

"Yes," Mother said.

Lottie asked, "What about the suicide note?"

"Typed on his computer," Mother said, "and left unsigned."

"And the book?" Myron asked. "How do you explain the pastor having *that* in his possession?"

She shrugged. "Planted by the real killer, who had taken it from the previous victim—John Miller."

The normally taciturn Wally spoke up. "What motive could there be for attacking Creed?"

"I have indeed arrived at one," Mother said, nodding. "But since it's merely conjecture at this juncture, I will keep it to myself . . . for now. Although I will give you a hint." Her smile looked a little crazed. "Binoculars."

The *Hawaii Five-O* theme began playing in her pocket.

Mother took the call, which was brief. "Yes. Right. Understood."

Returning the phone to her pocket, she gestured to me. "Come, Brandy. I'm needed back at the church."

Mother was on the move, heading toward the door, and I fell in behind her.

"*Sheriff!*" Myron called out after us. "What are *we* supposed to do?"

"Stay available," Mother said over her shoulder.

After a few blocks, we parted company, Mother striding toward the church while I continued on to the Pullman, definitely *not* striding.

It was around four o'clock, Sushi's suppertime, which used to be six, when we had ours. But over the years she had pushed it back to five-thirty, and when she got away with that, to five o'clock, and it's only a matter of time till it's three.

Anyway, I took Soosh outside, then put her food down, and when she'd finished, gave her a shot of insulin. She always got a treat for taking the needle, so I had bought extra doggie cookies for that purpose. And even though they were tucked back in a sack on the counter out of her view, she had (as Mother had noted) a nose like a bloodhound and barked up at where they were.

I was hungry enough to eat a doggie cookie myself, but instead I microwaved a frozen tuna casserole and ate it over the sink. Elegant, I know. Then I went back to the parlor, moved the chalkboard away from the couch, lay down, and fell asleep, taking a whole three or four seconds to do so.

A loud clap of thunder woke me to darkness, rain pummeling the roof of the train car. I reached for my cell resting on the floor: 9:36. I turned on a lamp and went to see if Mother was in the bedroom, thinking she had come back and not wanted to wake me.

But she wasn't here.

Returning to the parlor, I was about to call her cell when the front door banged open as if the wind had done it. But a drenched Mother blew in, along with rain and more wind.

"What a storm!" she declared. She was dripping, her hair hanging like seaweed.

"Where have you been?" I asked. "You had me worried."

"No need to fret, dear. I finished up with the Burlington team—they're a lot nicer than ours, by the by—and then I had supper at the diner."

I gestured to the soggy sack in her hand. "That for me?"

"If you like. It's what's left of what I ate—a little goulash and half a roll."

"Thanks. But I had something already."

I took the sack and put it in the fridge. Meanwhile, Mother was making a puddle on the carpet.

"You should get out of those wet clothes," I said. "And then we can talk."

Shortly, she returned wearing pj's under her favorite pick chenille bathrobe with shoulder pads (from the forties, not eighties), which she refused to part with.

Mother joined me on the couch. Sushi, not to be left out, curled up between us.

"What's new?" I asked, wearily, somewhat groggy from the long nap.

Mother tucked her legs beneath her, creating a few stray pops. "Not much. It will take time to get any fingerprint results back from the 'suicide' paper, and the book as well. I've had an update from your boyfriend on Pastor Creed's condition, which has improved with a breathing tube, though the man remains unconscious."

"CT scan?"

She nodded. "No apparent damage to the brain . . . but inconclusive. He may *never* wake up. Which would surely please our killer."

I tucked my legs up under myself too. Nothing popping yet.

"Mother, I've been thinking. We've been trying to connect all these attacks to one person."

"Or two, working in tandem."

"But what if there were *multiple* killers, not working in tandem but independent of one another."

Mother frowned. "Go on, dear."

I got off the couch, located the eraser, crouched before the chalkboard, and wiped away everything under the motive/opportunity columns, leaving only the names of the victims and suspects.

"What if," I said, "Pastor Creed really did kill Morella— for blackmailing him over their affair, or because she took up with someone else, or possibly some other reason. And suppose Wally believed the mayor had killed Morella, to hide an affair that could've destroyed the Hatcher marriage. Wally, inspired by Morella's Poe-like killing, might have tried, unsuccessfully, to kill Myron. Meanwhile, Paula, upset by the sudden appearance of Miller, aka Phillips, her old partner-in-crime, saw an opportunity to dispatch the ex-con in another Poe-like way."

Mother was now seated on the edge of the couch, leaning forward. She wasn't nodding, but her eyes were narrowed. "And how does it all come back around to Pastor Creed?"

"Well, that's where I'm stuck," I admitted. "Paula could have gotten the book from Miller, to plant with the suicide letter . . . but that *couldn't* be, because we were with her when Creed was hanged." I paused. "Here's an idea . . . Paula and Wally got together and conspired to kill and frame Creed. She gave Wally the book, and he did the deed."

Mother said, "But Wally only found out about Morella and Creed this afternoon at the meeting."

"Did he? What if Paula knew and used that information to recruit Wally, insinuating that the pastor killed his daughter?"

"Dear, you may have it," Mother said, getting to her feet. "But I'm going to have to sleep on your theory—I'm knackered, as the Brits say." She was so tired, she didn't bother saying that in her UK accent. "We'll explore all your excellent theories some more in the morning."

Sushi trotted after Mother, preferring the comfortable bed to my couch-bound presence.

Not bothering to change into pj's, I turned out the light and curled up.

Outside the rain was pouring, the wind howling, rattling the windows and shaking the Pullman. With all that clamor, I didn't think I could fall asleep, my mind still buzzing around possible solutions to my theory. But the rocking of the train car from the wind and the drumming of the rain were actually lulling. Even the breathy, wolflike howl of it served to soothe me. . . .

Sushi woke me up, licking my face. Which only momentarily startled me, because that was what she always did when she had to piddle. In the dark, I looked at my cell phone—3:13—and groaned.

"Can't you wait?" I asked her, and tried to stuff the little dog under my blanket, but she wiggled out.

I got up, joined Sushi at the front door, opened it, and she scurried out onto the platform and down the few stairs.

I followed, glad that the rain had stopped, a half moon glowing and a few stars shining between dark clouds.

But when I stepped to the ground, something was wrong. My feet had landed funny. And nothing looked familiar.

Was I dreaming?

I couldn't make out any streetlights, and where was the driveway? But there was no driveway, no Explorer, and no house! Only trees and train tracks extending into the dark horizon. The Train That Went Nowhere had gone somewhere!

In the distance I heard a lonesome whistle blow, like the old song says. Then it blew again, louder, and I for one did not feel at all lonesome. I only wished I did!

We were sitting on the main line tracks!

I yelled to Sushi, who came scampering up a slope, and grabbed her, ran up the stairs and inside, then down the narrow hallway and into the bedroom.

"Wake up!" I screamed at Mother.

She bolted upright. "What? Where?"

As I threw back her covers, the train whistled again, sounding way too close.

"We've got to go or we're dead!" I shouted.

With Sushi tucked under one arm, I grabbed Mother with the other, pulling her roughly out of bed.

"Move, move, move!" I yelled.

As I shoved her toward the bedroom's exit door, Mother reached out and snatched her glasses off the nightstand.

Then we were outside, on the rear platform. But at this end, there were no stairs.

"Jump!" I commanded.

Befuddled, she hesitated, so I jumped holding Sushi, pulling her along with us, and we tumbled onto the hard gravel on the track.

The train whistle was earsplitting, the roar of its powerful engine unmistakable, Mother now fully cognizant of the danger.

Grabbing on to each other, we scrambled off the track and tumbled down into a wet, weedy gully just seconds before the train collided with the Pullman.

A Trash 'n' Treasures Tip

One ploy a dishonest Internet bookseller will do is to trim the edges of a book jacket or a paperbound edition, where most wear and tear occurs, to make it seem a better copy in a photograph. Mother fell for this once. The cover of her Avon 1958 paperback edition of *The Case of the Red Box* just says *Red Box* at the top—a very tricky trick on the bookseller's part, since the book's real title is *The Red Box* and *The Case of* was added on the paperback.

Chapter Eleven

Poe Dough

The Pullman exploded into so much flying kindling on impact with the train, the crunching and snapping of wood accompanied by the screech of metal wheels braking against sparking metal tracks.

As the debris came raining down, I covered Sushi, and Mother covered me. Luckily, most of the projectiles had been propelled forward, away from us, and what did hit was splintered wooden shards and nothing metallic.

Slowly, we unfurled ourselves.

"Well, *that* wasn't reminiscent of any Poe work I know of!" Mother said as if mildly outraged, sitting up with her legs out in front of her, straightening her cockeyed glasses.

"Are you okay?" I asked.

She nodded. "In one piece, apparently. *You,* dear?"

I took stock of myself. Other than a scraped knee and a few cuts on my bare feet, I appeared intact.

Mother asked urgently, "And little Sushi?"

I nodded. Sushi seemed unharmed, too, though her expression asked, *What was* that *all about?*

Above us a God-like voice boomed, *"Anyone down there?"*

But the figure with a flashlight, standing above us, was decidedly earthly, if silhouetted dramatically against the night sky.

"Two of us!" I called out.

"And a dog!" Mother added.

We were both still sitting on the grass amid smoking debris.

The figure descending the slope proved to be a man in a cap, denim shirt, and overalls.

Mother and I squinted as his light beam passed over us. He asked with gruff concern, "You girls all right?"

"I believe we have all our parts," Mother said, "and they appear to still be connected to us."

He helped us to our feet, Mother first.

"What *was* that we hit?" he asked. "Not a car?"

"A *railroad* car," I said. "Not auto-type car."

His eyes were large now. "You were *inside?*"

"Dear," Mother said to him, "might I suggest we discuss this in your engine cab? Over coffee, perhaps?"

"Why, yes—of course."

He assisted Mother up the slope; I followed with Sushi in my arms. The little darling's expression continued to raise the question of how and why we humans got into such messes.

While we walked alongside the stopped train, our rescuer introduced himself as Lionel Erickson, the engineer, and Mother introduced us as the sheriff of Serenity County and her deputy, and did anyone ever point out to him how "Lionel" was the name of the famous model trains?

"First time today," he said.

When we'd reached the red Canadian Pacific engine, I asked Mr. Erickson if this train would be safe sitting here on the tracks, and the engineer said he'd notified the National

Response Center right after the impact to shut down this line.

The cramped interior of the cab included two padded chairs on small risers in front of the double windshields, the one on the right facing a control panel with switches and gauges and a built-in phone; the one on the left, for a co-engineer (none on this trip, apparently), had a small work area.

Soon, Mother was seated in the latter chair, and Erickson was in his, swiveled toward her. I perched behind them in a little jump seat with Sushi on my lap. Her attitude had changed to interest, as this was a whole new setting for her. And us, for that matter.

With the cab's lights on, I got a better look at our host: midthirties, handsome and studious in his dark-framed glasses. He seemed a more likely engineer of buildings than trains.

"Where are we?" I asked.

"About five miles north of Antiqua," he said. "What were you doing in a boxcar on the tracks, anyway?"

"Not a boxcar," Mother said. "Although I've often dreamed of what it might have been like to ride the rails and eat beans from a can warmed over a fire, but that would seem dangerous in a wooden boxcar, wouldn't it?"

"Mother. Stay on point."

She nodded. Her glasses, still slightly off-center, jiggled. "A Pullman car is what we were in."

He frowned, blinked. "What?"

"An old Pullman turned into lodging as part of a bed-and-breakfast, although frankly breakfast appears more an honorary designation in this instance."

"Mother . . ." I said. Maybe she'd been shaken up worse than I realized.

But Erickson was nodding. "Ah! That converted Pullman over in Antiqua?"

"Exactly, dear," Mother said, nodding. "That's where my daughter and I were staying."

"I thought she was your deputy."

"She's both. Brandy is a versatile young lady."

He smiled, chuckled. "You know, I stayed there once with my wife, in that Pullman. She's into antiquing, weekend getaway. But how in the world did it get onto this track?"

I said, "Someone must have pushed us during the night. Maybe with a car. Auto, not Pullman."

"Apparently," Mother added ominously, "someone wishing to do us harm."

You think?

"Well, whoever did it," Lionel said, "they went to a lot of trouble manually switching the track, then back again." He shook his head slowly. "A pity. All that beautiful woodwork and those lovely antiques . . . destroyed. What a loss. My wife will cry. Ah . . . but at least you're okay."

I was just beginning to wonder if we rated. "What happens now?" I asked.

"The dispatcher at the CAC will by now have contacted the Accident Analysis Branch," he said, "and they'll be sending a cleanup crew and notifying the Federal Railroad Association to see if they want to get involved." He paused. "The FRA usually won't send investigators unless there's a death, or derailment . . . but they may want to get involved in this. It's a crime—attempted homicide. But I've never heard of a train being used as a murder weapon before."

Mother said, "You simply *must* watch *Double Indemnity* sometime, dear."

Glumly, I asked, "Then we have to stay here?"

"Yes. Sorry. I'll do my best to make you ladies as comfortable as I can."

Mother asked about coffee, which Lionel was able to

provide, and I inquired about a place to lie down, which he couldn't provide, because sleeping or even napping on the job was not permitted. But I was informed of a small padded bench I could use, across from the lavatory in the back of the engine.

Mother, sipping java from a thermos lid: "So, tell me, Lionel—may I call you Lionel?" She didn't wait for a confirmation. "How long have you wanted to be a train engineer? Ever since you got your first toy trains as a boy?"

His eyes sparkled behind the glasses. "How did you guess?"

"I can just picture how wide your young eyes became when you saw the words 'Lionel Trains' on, what? The classic Blue Streak set?"

"I never had any Lionel trains."

"Oh?" she said, disappointed.

"But," the engineer said, "my parents gave me a Brio set when I was three."

How could Mother engage in such small talk after what just happened to us? Or should I say, how could I expect her not to?

I vacated the jump seat, handed the furry little package that was Sushi to Mother, went through the small passageway to the back, located the airplane-style bathroom, used it, found the little bench, and made like a pretzel.

Later, the muffled voices of the cleanup crew outside woke me, and I unwound myself. Crikey, my neck! (Do not read the prior remark in a UK accent, please.)

I wandered back to the cab, early morning sunshine streaming through the double front windows now. Ahead, workmen were walking the line, Erickson among them, looking for stray debris, most of it having already been cleared from the tracks.

Mother, in the engineer's chair, looked up from reading a thick manual, with no greeting.

"I believe I could operate this train," she announced. She wiggled her shodden feet. "Look, dear—I've gotten back my shoes and duty belt!"

She looked comical in the pink robe with the bulky belt cinched at her waist. Her badge had been found as well—the five-pointed blue-trimmed gold star was pinned to the chenille garment.

It made me glad I'd slept in my clothes, although by now they weren't exactly fresh.

"Any sign of my sandals?" I asked.

"Not so far."

"How about our cell phones?"

She shook her head, then gestured to the flat counter in front of the co-engineer's chair. "Have some fresh donuts and coffee that the nice men brought."

I hoisted myself into the seat, then reached for an old-fashioned.

"How much longer till we're sprung?" I asked, chewing.

"Not until we're cleared to move. Then Lionel is going to drop us at the crossing at Antiqua, which is just a hop, skip, and a jump to the bed-and-breakfast—rather, the site of what once was the B-and-B, that is."

I groused, "I'm not hopping, skipping, or jumping *any-where* in bare feet."

Mother put the manual down in her lap. "Dear, you can wear my shoes."

You would bet, when the time came, that I'd take her up on that.

I asked, "Can't *someone* give us a ride?"

"We *are* getting a ride, darling girl, on this train."

"And then we walk."

"And then we walk," she agreed.

"*Fine,*" I said, sounding like the whiny teenager she often reduced me to. "Do you have the extra key to the Explorer?" My set was in my purse, probably in Timbuktu by now.

Where *is* Timbuktu, anyway?

Mother patted a pocket on the belt. "Right here."

She meant the keys, not Timbuktu.

I looked around, frowning, mildly panicked. "Where's Sushi?"

"The little darling is off helping us find our things."

I started to get out of the chair, "Oh, I don't know if that's such a good idea—she's not exactly Rin Tin Tin."

Mother waved me back. "Sit, sit, sit. She's fine. Having a lovely time."

Glad someone was.

Erickson climbed into the cab, followed by Sushi, who had one of my sandals in her mouth. She trotted over and dropped it at my feet.

"Good girl," I said. One was better than none.

"I've been given the okay to go," he told us. "Are you sure you don't want one of the men from the cleanup crew to drive you over to Antiqua in one of the trucks?"

"No," Mother said, simultaneously with my "Yes."

"Thank you all the same," she said, smiling but firm.

"Well, all right, if that's what you prefer."

Mother remained seated in his chair. "Lionel, dear," she cooed, coquettishly. "Mightn't I drive the train? Just for this teensy while? With your supervision, of course! I've read the manual cover to cover, twice."

So that's why she didn't want a lift back.

"I'm afraid," Erickson said, "that would be against regulations. Company *and* federal."

She batted her eyelashes, which twitched like a spider's legs behind the magnified lenses. "I *am* the county sheriff, after all. If we were caught, you could blame me. You could say I commandeered the vehicle!"

"Ah . . ." He looked to me for help.

I might have informed him that Mother wasn't licensed to drive a car, although she would only say that her revoked license said nothing about locomotives. Loco was right.

So I merely smiled.

You see, I just love these situations. Look forward to them. To watching people squirm when they get caught in Mother's web (the eyelashes should have been a warning). Or, to put it succinctly, welcome to my world.

"All right," Lionel said with a sigh. "But I'll be right next to you."

"One question," Mother asked, as she swiveled to face the control panel.

"Yes?"

"Might I wear your cap?"

I settled into the co-engineer's chair with Sushi, noting the lack of a seat belt. Wouldn't it be just my luck, and Sushi's, too, to narrowly escape being hit by a train only to get derailed on the trip to safety?

But you know what? Mother turned out to be a pretty decent engineer, driver's license or not—although she overdid it a little with the whistle approaching the crossroad. And pouted, at the end, when she had to give the cap back.

We bid our new, somewhat bemused friend good-bye, Lionel promising to make sure any more of our belongings that turned up would be sent to us. From there it was a short jaunt (I wore the one sandal and one of Mother's shoes) to the Explorer, which she unlocked and climbed into. From the passenger's seat she used the radio transmitter to call Deputy Chen.

While she was doing that, I revisited where the Pullman used to sit, Sushi tagging along.

The ground was muddy from the overnight rain, revealing tire tracks leading up to the train tracks. But I doubted any usable castings could be made, because the rain had continued through the night and obliterated details.

Sushi and I returned to Mother.

"Hop in, dear," she said, just a woman of a certain age in a pink chenille robe who was sitting in a police vehicle. She might have been just your average everyday, run-of-the-mill mental patient, escaped from an institution and recovered by the cops. "I want to see if Myron is at city hall."

I handed her Sushi, then came around and got behind the wheel.

As we drove the few blocks, Mother told me that in addition to filling in Deputy Chen, she had also reached Tony, who'd be returning to Antiqua as soon as possible.

"That's all he said?" I asked, disappointed that he apparently hadn't expressed concern for our latest narrow escape.

"Well," she said, "naturally, he was relieved we were all right. He was so droll."

"Droll?"

"Yes, he said something about wringing my neck. Isn't he a stitch?"

At city hall we found the door locked, but just as we were about to return to the SUV, a plump woman in a white blouse, navy shirt, and jacket ran up to us.

"Ah," Mother said to me, "here's the bank manager. I don't believe you've met."

But we skipped the introductions, as the woman, out of breath, addressed Mother. "Am I ever glad to see *you!*"

The fact that the sheriff was dressed for bed didn't seem to faze her.

"Why, Gladys," Mother said, "what has you in such a tizzy?"

"The bank has been robbed!"

Frowning, Mother said, amazingly calm, "When, dear?"

For all the bank manager's urgency, I didn't hear any alarms ringing.

"Well, I don't know exactly," she said. "But some time after we closed at noon on Saturday."

So maybe a little late for alarms.

I asked, "Don't the vaults have a time lock?"

"Well, of course," Gladys said, "but it wasn't the main vault that was robbed, it was the night depository safe. All the bags are gone!"

We drove right over to the bank, Gladys sitting in back, like a prisoner.

Soon we were seated in the woman's office, with her behind the desk, where a nameplate identified her as the bank manager, her last name GOOCH. Mother and I were in chairs opposite her, as if we were there for a loan. Sushi was roaming free within the closed-off office. With luck she wouldn't make a deposit.

Gladys explained, "I got here about half an hour ago, to open up. The first thing I do is unlock the night depository safe and remove all the bags that have been stored there over the weekend."

"Who," Mother asked, "besides yourself, has the combination?"

"No one."

"Then how could the safe have been opened?"

She looked at me, frustrated by my lack of knowledge of her world. "It didn't! The bags were removed from the *outside,* not the inside."

Mother frowned. "How is that possible?"

"It's call 'fishing,'" I said, showing them both that I knew more than either one thought I did. "Somebody with a key to the night depository opens the hatch outside and then uses a rope with a hook to pull all the bags out."

That made Mother smile. "Simple, but ingenious," she marveled. "Does a security camera cover the depository outside?"

Gladys shook her head. "Only inside the bank. The

night deposit is in front, and the only outside camera is in the alley."

Bet that was going to change.

Mother asked, "Can you determine how much was taken?"

Her sigh came long and deep. "No, because this was an unusually busy weekend for all the businesses, completely atypical . . . except, of course, for fest weekend, once a year."

"It seems to me," Mother said, "the thief would be interested only in the *cash* in those bags—that's where the loss is. The checks will probably be ditched."

Gladys nodded. "And checks can be reissued. And, of course, any debit and credit cards that were used for payment aren't affected."

Mother frowned in thought. "Do all the businesses use the night depository?"

"Not all," Gladys said, "but most."

"And how many keys are each user given?"

"One per customer. We don't want them floating around."

Mother nodded. "Did anyone notify you of a missing key?"

"No," Gladys said. Then she thought a moment and added, "Wait—Lottie Everhart called me Thursday morning, after her shop and all the others were broken into, and said that her key was missing . . . but then she called back later and said she'd recovered it. She'd apparently dropped it on the floor."

Firmly, Mother said, "I need a list of everyone who has a night deposit key."

Gladys nodded and exited the office, Sushi watching her go.

I turned to Mother. "Don't you need to notify the FBI? This is an FDIC bank."

"Soon, dear."

"Mother!"

"Let's not get ahead of ourselves. I need all the details first."

Gladys was back, handing Mother a printout.

I stood and looked over her shoulder.

Such familiar names as Myron Hatcher, Lottie Everhart, Paula Baxter, and Wally Thorp were included on the list. Oddly, Rick Wheeler was not.

Mother zeroed in on that. "Rick Wheeler doesn't use the night depository?"

"No. He has his own safe."

"I'll want to hold on to this," Mother said, indicating the paper.

"Certainly," Gladys replied. "I've made another copy for the FBI, who should be here soon."

Mother stiffened. "Oh. You've already called them?"

"Of course." Gladys blinked. "Called them first thing. Standard procedure in a bank robbery."

Mother, obviously miffed, asked, "Then why involve me?"

The bank manager shrugged. "I thought you should know. You *are* the sheriff."

Mother stood abruptly. "I am indeed. When they arrive, you may tell the FBI that I've begun my own investigation. We can't be sitting on our hands in a matter like this. Come, Brandy."

Out on the sidewalk, Mother in her pink robe was getting curious looks from a few pedestrians.

"The Fibbies are going to ruin everything!" she blurted.

"The what?"

"The Fibbies! The FBI! The Feds! They're going to come in and take over, and send yours truly packing!"

I'd rarely seen her so distressed and couldn't help feeling sorry for her.

I looked down at Sushi in my arms. "I have an idea. . . ."

"A cunning plan?"

We were both fans of Blackadder, whose catchphrase that was.

"A cunning plan," I confirmed.

Leaving the car in front of the bank, I led Mother up the street to the bakery in the next block and then told her to wait outside with Sushi.

George, arranging pastries inside the glass display case, straightened as I barged in.

I asked, "Did you use the bank's night depository yesterday?"

"Yes," he said. "Why? Is something wrong?"

"I need a little sack with a few doggie cookie crumbs inside—no cookies, just crumbs."

He winced, as if he were deaf and I was speaking too softly. "What?"

I repeated the request. Distinctly.

George hesitated but complied. As I was leaving, he called out, "What *about* the night depository?"

"Stay tuned," I said.

I rejoined Mother, who took the sack and looked into it.

She frowned. "*This* is supposed to lift me from the doldrums?"

"Every time George gives me back my change," I explained, "it has either frosting or crumbs on it. *His* bag was in the depository." I shook the closed little sack. "*This* has crumbs."

Mother's grin was downright wolfish. She was right with me.

"Dear," she said, "if ever I thought you were of merely average intelligence, you have proven me wrong!"

"Thank you . . . ?"

She continued, "I don't believe the thief would risk hiding the bags in his home. But he might think his *business* is a safe haven. Let's start on the left side of Antiques Drive and work our way down the street, then go up on the right."

We crossed over to Top Drawer and entered.

Myron, feather-dusting his treasures, went bug-eyed when he got a gander of Mother in her beddie-bye getup.

"Sheriff, what in . . . ?" he began, duster going limp in his hand.

She approached him. "Mayor, you simply won't *believe* what happened to us last night!" A hand behind her back gestured for me to get going.

I conveyed Sushi to the back of the store, set her down, let her sniff inside the sack, and said, singsongy, "Find the *cook*-ie!"

She just *loved* to play hiding games. Her eyes looked like shiny new pennies, and her tongue lolled as she panted with anticipation.

The little furball took off like a greyhound chasing a metal rabbit, sniffing everywhere, jumping up on everything she could, and what she couldn't reach—say, an armoire—I held her up to sniff on top.

When we came across the basement door, I sent her down there. Ditto with the access to the attic. Both off-limits areas got no reaction.

Sushi worked her way to the front, where Mother remained holding Myron's attention.

He was saying, "Now the *night depository* has been robbed? Sheriff, things have really gotten out of hand. I'm glad *I* didn't use it this weekend—most of my transactions were electronic, and what cash I took in went home with me. Meaning no offense, but don't you need outside help at this point?"

"The FBI is on the way," she replied, as if it were she who'd summoned them. "And they'll want to talk to everyone who has a key to the depository."

Myron's eyebrows went up and down. "That's about every business in town," he said.

Impatient to get going, I gave Mother a little nudge.

Abruptly she said, "Well, must run. Places to go, people to arrest! Toodles!"

The next stop was Paula's Relics Antiques, where we repeated the same routine. I was sure Sushi would sniff out George's bag here, because of Paula's past bank robbery conviction—but no sale.

Nor did Lottie's Somewhere in Time get us anywhere.

We continued on to Junk 'n' Stuff, where Wally's mounds of rubble seemed the perfect place to hide the bank bags, and the most difficult for Sushi to suss out. But the little beast loved clambering over hill and dale, and when she discovered a partially eaten bagel beneath a pile of toppled magazines, I could only marvel at her thorough resourcefulness. Still, we moved on because, well, a bagel isn't a cookie.

We tried another half-dozen shops, unsuccessfully, but when we got to Rick's Treasure Aisles, the barn door was padlocked.

"What now?" I asked Mother.

"What else? We go in. I'm the sheriff."

"But we don't have a warrant."

"We have probable cause!"

"Do we?"

"Deputies should be seen and not heard."

From her belt, Mother retrieved her two little picks and had the padlock off in a few seconds.

We went in, closing the barn door behind us.

The ground floor with its many dealer booths would be an unlikely place for the bank bags to be hidden—among other things, it risked one such dealer running across the swag. But the wraparound balcony—storage for such salvaged items as old doors, window frames, lattices, and iron works—would offer any number of perfect hiding places, since the items could be viewed from below and thus had far less foot traffic.

I steered Sushi to the wooden steps leading upward, put the sack under her nose, let her sniff, and said the magic word: *cookie.*

From below, Mother and I watched as the little devil climbed to the balcony, then began weaving in and out and around the bulky items, disappearing, reappearing.

Then . . . a muffled bark.

Sushi kept yapping until Mother and I found her behind a leaning door, where an old steamer trunk had been tucked. I tugged the heavy piece out into the open and bowed down before it.

A SOLD sign was taped to the trunk, by way of discouraging any would-be customer. The lid had a hole-mounted lock, which needed a corrugated key to open, and I was about to ask Mother if her picks would work when company arrived.

"What the hell are you doing?" demanded Rick, who had come up behind Mother.

She whirled. "Ah! Mr. Wheeler. Sorry you weren't here when we arrived."

Rick stepped closer to her. "You have no right breaking into my store."

His demeanor was threatening enough that Sushi growled, and I got to my feet.

Mother pulled herself up. "Perhaps you forget that I'm the sheriff."

He looked her up and down. "You could've fooled me. What is this, a slumber party that got out of hand?"

"No. It's something else that got out of hand. The bank's night depository was robbed last night, and I'm checking each and every business."

Rick sneered. "I don't even *use* the bank depository. I have my *own* safe."

"Then perhaps you'll help us cross you off the list by opening this trunk."

"Why *that* trunk?"

"I have reason to believe it may contain the stolen deposit bags. Probable cause, as we say in the law enforcement game. Now, I'd like the key to this trunk, or else I'll have to break into it . . . and I'd hate to damage such a lovely piece, in such fine condition."

"You're wasting your time, lady."

"Then prove me wrong." Mother held out a hand. "The key, Mr. Wheeler."

Rick sighed. His body seemed to deflate like a punctured inner tube. From the front pocket of his jeans, he removed a small key and placed it in Mother's outstretched palm.

She passed it to me, and I opened the trunk. Within nestled the stolen Wells Fargo depository bags.

Sushi had her front paws on the rim of the trunk, nose twitching. She looked at the bags, then accusingly at me: *So where's the cookie, already?*

"You'll have all the cookies you want, later," I assured her, patting her head. She frowned but allowed herself to be plucked back into my arms.

Mother was removing handcuffs from a duty belt pocket on her robe. "Turn around, Mr. Wheeler."

"How did you figure it?" he asked, complying.

"Took crumbs to catch a crumb, dear," Mother said. "Now, let's go downstairs, shall we?"

On the ground floor, Mother put the handcuffed Rick in a chair at the checkout counter.

Mother said, "Here's how I see it. You were behind the break-ins on Wednesday night. You needed a key to the night depository and found one in Lottie's store, made a copy, went back the next morning during business hours, and dropped it on the floor."

Rick said nothing, looking past her.

"Why go to all that trouble?" I asked him. "Weren't you dating Lottie? You could've gotten that key an easier way."

Rick thought for a while. Maybe he realized his rights hadn't been read to him and decided it wouldn't hurt him to answer. Anyway, he sighed, laughed . . . and talked.

"I wanted the break-ins to seem as if some local was looking to find the Poe prize early," he said. "And I've never gone out with Lottie—we're friendly only because of her husband, who was a buddy of mine."

"A buddy *only?*" I asked.

He scoffed. "What, have you been listening to women who want to go out with me but I turn down? Yes, he was only a friend."

"Who killed himself in a very Poe-like manner," I said. "Don't you find that odd?"

Rick smiled a little. "Not to me. Mike had a very twisted sense of humor, even as bummed out as he was over that Poe Folly fiasco. Going the Poe route was his way of commenting on what happened to him. And, anyway, he hated that damn cat."

Mother asked, "How long had you been planning to rob the night depository?"

He sighed. "Not that long. I mean, I never would have considered it at all, except business has been lousy. The rent from dealers just isn't enough, and last time I raised it, just a little, I lost a bunch of them. Then I got to thinking about all the cash that got collected on fest weekend and would have to be deposited. I figured I'd be above suspicion, you know, ruled out? Because I didn't use the depository service and you'd need a key to pull that stunt."

Mother nodded. "Nicely reasoned. Too bad you didn't put your brain power to more positive use. And, of course, you didn't count on the presence of Sheriff Vivian J. Borne, or the abilities of a certain bloodhound with a penchant for pastry."

Rick frowned. "Huh?"

"Now," Mother said, "about these *murders* . . ."

That startled Rick, his eyebrows rising, his eyes widening, showing white all around.

"Hold on, lady! You're not going to pin those on me! I didn't kill *anybody*. I'll cop to robbery but not *murder*. What kind of a monster do you take me for? I wouldn't hurt Myron or Pastor Creed, and I barely *knew* Morella . . . and that guy who found the book, I never met him at all. That book, by the way, that thing was a fake all the way."

Mother's brow knit a sweater. She asked, "What makes you say the book wasn't authentic?"

He smirked, grunted a laugh. "Well, for one thing, Myron never gave us a chance to examine it. And for another thing? After we drew slips where it should be hidden? I looked in the wastebasket where our glorious mayor had thrown them, and *every one* was for Top Drawer—*his* store."

Stunned by this revelation, I asked, "Why didn't you *say* anything?"

He looked at me, sighed, shook his head. "Because, frankly, honey, I was relieved. I didn't want a frenzied mob descending on my place, messing up all the booths . . . which the dealers would have to straighten up later."

Outside, car doors slammed. The barn door opened and in came two men in sunglasses and crisp navy suits, a blue tie on one white shirt and a red tie on the other.

"Have you seen the sheriff?" the taller of the pair asked our little group.

"Present and accounted for," Mother replied.

The agent removed his shades for a better look at the woman in the pink robe.

"*You're* the sheriff?" he asked.

Mother tugged on the badge pinned to chenille. "Yes indeedy diddey do. And you are?"

"Ah . . . the FBI."

"Good. Thank you for your assistance." She gestured to Rick. "Well, here's your bank robber, gentlemen, and you'll find the missing bags in a trunk upstairs."

The agents traded surprised expressions.

I pointed out the trunk above.

"Now," Mother went on, "I simply must scoot. We can confer later. At the moment I have a murderer to catch."

She breezed by the pair, and I followed with Sushi, flashing them my best smile.

Outside, I said, "After all this . . . *Myron* is our man?"

"Indeed."

We hoofed it back to the bank to get the Explorer, my mind abuzz, then I drove us to Top Drawer, where a CLOSED sign hung on the door.

"Try his residence," Mother said.

I headed south out of town.

"What makes you so sure it's him?" I asked.

"Something Rick said, dear, makes things finally fall into place. Specifically, what he said about eliminating himself as a suspect in the robbery."

I nodded. "You think Myron hoped to do the same thing by making himself one of the victims, but one who'd luckily survived."

"Luck had nothing to do with it. He dropped that key fob by his Caddy so we'd know something was wrong and go looking for him." She paused. "And he walked into that church basement willingly, although not alone, and *that* is what Pastor Creed saw through his binoculars—

and I'll wager His Honor he wasn't in that 'tomb' nearly as long as we assumed."

I nodded. "And Creed figured he could use that knowledge to get funding for the new church, *and* parsonage, which explains the scripture reading. To let Myron know what the good pastor had witnessed, but that he was no threat."

"Exactly. At least as long as the mayor helped him with that funding."

"But who walled Myron up?"

"His accomplice, John Miller. Remember the mortar residue found in his hotel room? Then Miller or rather *Phillips*, became a loose end, or perhaps got greedy. Turn here!"

I did. "Boy, *everybody* was putting the squeeze on the mayor! But what's behind all the Poe allusions? And did he kill Morella, too?"

"Yes, dear, but for now just swing in there."

We were at the Hatchers' driveway. I pulled in and up behind Caroline's burgundy Buick sedan. The Caddy was not there, but she might know where to find her husband.

I cracked a window for Sushi, leaving her behind as we climbed out. When I skirted around the sedan, I saw that the front bumper was badly dented.

Mother noticed it too.

"Maybe it's not *Mr.* Hatcher we want," I said, "but *Mrs.* Hatcher! Maybe she's been protecting him all along, cleaning up after him."

Mother shook her head. "No. I'm sure Myron merely used *her* car to push the Pullman."

The front door of the looming house opened and a distraught Caroline ran out. She was in a robe, too, but a flowing white silk one, like something from the cover of a Gothic romance.

"He's *gone!*" she sobbed. "Myron's gone. I didn't *know!*
I swear I didn't *know!*"

"Which way?" Mother asked urgently.

Caroline pointed south.

"How long ago?"

"No more than five minutes," she said.

"Let's roll, Brandy!"

We reached the Explorer, but I paused at the driver's
side door. Behind us stood the woman, the Addams Family
house hovering over her, as she slumped there covering her
face with her hands.

As I gripped the door handle, I wasn't sure I was convinced; it might be a performance. "You're going to *believe* her, Mother?"

"Must I drive myself?" Mother demanded.

We got back into the Explorer and took pursuit, Mother
initiating the siren and flashing lights. Then she radioed in a
10-80 giving our position, all the while urging me to go
faster.

Rolling hills flattened into farmland. On a long, straight
stretch of highway, I could make out a vehicle in the distance, fleeing toward the horizon.

Within a few minutes, I had cut the miles between us
and the silver car.

"You're *gaining* on him!" Mother said, holding Sushi
tightly. "Good girl!"

I wasn't sure whether she meant me or Sushi.

Something else became clearer in the distance—a long
freight train, traveling horizontally at a good clip. It would
soon intersect with the highway.

"Can't you drive any faster?" Mother asked snippily.

"I'm going as fast as I dare," I snapped.

Snip: "If he makes it to that crossing, and we don't,
we've lost him."

Snap: "I'm not risking our lives over this! He's not going to get away with this."

Snip: "I know he's not, but I want to be the one who *sees* he doesn't!"

Ahead, Myron was traveling at a speed admittedly much more reckless than mine in a desperate attempt to make the crossing, where red lights were flashing, and to beat the train there.

But he didn't.

Nor could he slow down in time.

Or could he have?

We watched as the Cadillac slammed into the side of an oil tanker car. I was slowing at a safe distance as the fireball blossomed and rose in a terrible beauty right out of Poe.

A Trash 'n' Treasures Tip

Devious booksellers will sometimes use software to enhance a photo of the book's cover in their ad, making the colors more vibrant, enabling them to charge more than the book is worth. Mother finds this use of Photoshop an outrageously dishonest one, although when it comes to shots of herself, she's fine with it.

Chapter Twelve

Poe Me a Merlot

The Friday morning following her (and my return) from Antiqua, Mother summoned Tony and me to her office in Serenity's modern jail building, which was next door to the police station.

As I probably mentioned once or twice or one hundred times, Mother loves the old *Perry Mason* TV show, relishing in particular those final scenes in Perry's office, where Perry and Della and Paul Drake are having coffee, and Della brings up something about the case she doesn't understand.

"Perry," she would say, "how did you know to do this or that?" Or "Perry, how could so-and-so have known about such and such?"

Well, this morning was Mother's version of the final scene in *The Case of the Raven Madman*, and she was playing Perry, Tony appeared as Paul, and I of course became Della. But along with the coffee, we were enjoying a Danish dessert called *valnodkage* (walnut cake) served on Haviland pink rose china with sterling silver forks, which she'd made me bring from home (cups, too) . . . just in case you thought that was standard issue at the county jail.

Mother liked to claim the *valnodkage* recipe as her own, but in reality she'd taken it, like a bath towel, from the Svendsen Grand Hotel in Copenhagen on a trip to Denmark in the late 1960s. Specifically, she had stolen it from the kitchen of the hotel's famed chef, who she may or may not have been romantically "reclined" with, as she sometimes said.

Anyway, here it is for your dining pleasure. (I'm sure the recipe was never copyrighted, and, besides, the hotel is no longer in business.) (I checked.)

Valnodkage

For the Cake:

⅔ cup butter, softened
⅔ cup sugar
3 large eggs
½ teaspoon vanilla extract
1 cup all-purpose flour
½ teaspoon baking powder
½ cup chopped walnuts

For the Glazing:

1 cup powdered sugar
1 Tablespoon water
1 teaspoon lemon juice
Walnut halves (for decoration)

Cream the butter and sugar until smooth. Add the eggs one at a time, beating after each one. Stir in the vanilla. Add the flour sifted with the baking powder, and mix well. Fold in the walnuts. Pour into a buttered loaf or funnel pan. Bake at 350° F about 35 to 45 minutes, until done. Invert cake on cake rack, and while cooling (cake, not the cook), mix together the ingredients of the glazing, except the walnuts. When completely cooled (again, cake, not cook) cover the top (the cake's, not yours) with the glaze mixture and decorate with walnut halves.

Yield: Eight servings

Della, seated on the side of Perry's desk in a form-fitting knit dress and high heels, her shapely legs crossed, asked, "How did Myron Hatcher come to know John Miller?"

Okay, okay—I was in a chair in front of the desk, in a wrinkled blouse, torn jeans, and ancient tennies. In my defense, I was still somewhat traumatized by our ordeal.

But not Mother, behind her desk in uniform, not a robe.

"That's an easy one, dear," she said. "Remember, Paula informed us she'd told Myron about her past association with Owen Phillips, aka John Miller, who was now an antiques dealer, almost certainly a shady one. The mayor contacted 'Miller' to find him a convincing forged Poe antique item. Miller came up with the bogus book, and together Hatcher and his accomplice pocketed the cash from the other council members."

"Which is not," Tony put in, wearing his standard office attire (see Chapter 8), "the only money the mayor helped himself to."

This was news to Mother. "Oh?"

"His Honor," Tony said dryly, "collected more donations for the church than was needed for the basement project, keeping the overage."

I asked, "How *is* the pastor doing?"

"Still in the hospital," Mother replied. "But he's come around. He's cognitive enough to deny that he was having an affair with Morella—she never visited him in his parsonage, he avows. That rumor came to us from Myron, remember? But Pastor Creed *did* confirm seeing the mayor enter the church basement on his own volition, with a stranger whom he identified in a photo as Miller."

I said, "Did Creed admit to blackmailing the mayor?"

"He doesn't see it that way. He calls sharing what he saw with Hatcher just information designed to encourage His Honor in helping fund a new church."

"*And* parsonage," I added. "Will the pastor be charged with extortion, do you think?"

"Unlikely," Tony said. "His cooperation in clearing this up will go a long way."

I frowned. "But why on earth did Myron kill Morella?"

Mother sat forward, tenting her fingers. "That young woman started the whole pendulum swinging, dear. While having an affair with Myron, she learned of the fake book and blackmailed her lover for money to get out of town."

"Is that a theory?" I asked.

Mother's eyebrows rose. "Morella finding out about the book and blackmailing Myron? Yes. But that they were lovers we've established. Morella's friend Willow came forward and said she knew about the affair but didn't say anything about it till now, not wanting to get involved. More cake, anyone?"

Tony declined. I didn't. I'd lost eight pounds in Antiqua, and my clothes didn't fit. Sort of refreshing, though, to have my wardrobe too big for a change.

"I had a chance," Tony said, "to talk to Myron's helper."

Mother was on her feet, refreshing our coffee cups.

I asked, "And what did Ryan have to say?"

"The Chief and I interviewed him together," Mother said, sitting back behind her desk again. "The young man is an *ex*-helper, now. Has quit Top Drawer, which right now isn't open for business, anyway. What Caroline Hatcher will do with it, who's to say? Anyway, that scuffle in the street between Miller and Oldfield over finding the Poe book? Ryan admits he didn't see who got to the faux Poe

Tales first but was pressured by Hatcher to say it was the former."

Tony nodded. "Otherwise, the scam might have been discovered."

I asked, "What did Caroline know?"

Mother smiled and nodded at Tony. "Why don't you take that one, Chief, as you were at the interview too."

I noticed, now that they were colleagues, she was no longer calling him "Chiefie."

Tony stifled a smile at her magnanimous gesture. "Neither your mother nor I have come up with any sign that Mrs. Hatcher was involved with the homicides. She may have *suspected* her husband, but that's both hard to prove and not really a crime, unless she actually aided and abetted. Anyway, there'll be no charges."

Deputy Chen knocked on the doorjamb and stuck his head in. "Reminder about your eleven o'clock luncheon with the Garden Club, Sheriff," he said.

Mother's nod was almost a bow. "Thank you, Charles. Say, would you mind if I called you Charlie? I'm such an Earl Derr Biggers fan!"

"Who? And, uh . . . Charles, please."

The forty-something deputy disappeared.

"Pity he doesn't embrace his heritage," Mother said. Then she sighed. "A lady who lunches! That's my life of late—Serenity's leading theatrical light now lowered to playing the rubber chicken circuit."

Tony got to his feet. "And I should get back. Thanks for the cake, Vivian. And, uh . . . good job with the case."

Mother beamed and blushed just a little. "Thank you, Chief Cassato. That means a great deal to me."

He smiled, nodded, then signaled to me he wanted my company.

"See you later, Mother."

But she was basking in her glory and barely noticed me slipping out into the hall.

In the lobby, we paused in front of the double glass entrance doors.

"Dinner tonight?" he asked.

"Where?"

"I'll provide the steaks if you bring a salad."

"Deal. What time?"

"Seven should be fine," he said.

"Sounds like a plan."

Even though I'd be spending the evening at Tony's rustic cabin, I took time getting ready to remind him I hadn't always been a hot mess in need of a hot shower.

But I took one, then got out my curler, blew the dust off, fired it up, styled my shoulder-length blond hair in loose waves, then applied the war paint.

(**Mother to Brandy:** Now who's politically incorrect?)

If you're not interested in my makeup or clothes, skip down to the paragraph beginning "Sushi, who always went with me to Tony's cabin . . ."

I don't buy a lot of makeup. I have only one mascara (Dior Addict It-Lash), one eye pencil (MAC, Bountiful Brown), one eye shadow (Chanel, Trace 86), one blush (NARS, Orgasm), and one lipstick (Chanel, 61 Bonheur). They're expensive, but less costly than a drawerful of mishaps, drying out in there and collecting bacteria.

My perfume is Juicy Couture's Viva La Juicy. I also have Norma Kamali's perfume, which she stopped making some time ago—a silver bottle with atomizer that came in a black velvet box—that on special occasions I'll spritz in the air, then walk through it, because the scent is so strong. But for tonight, I used Juicy.

My ensemble was a black eyelet cotton dress by Velvet

(end of last year sale), black and gold floral necklace by Kate Spade (outlet); and white Rag & Bone platform sandals (sold cheap on eBay by a dissatisfied owner)—but I wasn't going to be on my feet that long. (Think what you like.) My purse was a little black Coach with funky decals that I'd waited for for months to go on sale (Von Maur).

Sushi, who always went with me to the cabin, was on the bed watching me get ready but evincing little interest, obviously assuming by what I was putting on that Tony's hideaway was not my destination.

So when I said, "Let's go to the cabin," she nearly did a backflip off the bed.

Downstairs, I had already gathered a picnic basket of ingredients for the salad—iceberg lettuce, homegrown tomatoes, green and red peppers, radishes, carrots, celery, and red onion. Also, freshly homemade Italian dressing.

Mother was at the home of one of her gal pals for a gathering of their mystery book club, the Red-Hatted League, and I left her a reminder of where Sushi and I would be. Then we headed out to the C-Max.

Tony lived out in the country, about fifteen miles north of Serenity, along a winding two-lane highway that hugged the banks of the picturesque Mississippi River. Right now, with the sun hanging low in a sky streaked with purple, the last rays of the day shimmered like diamonds on the water. Holding Sushi tight on my lap, I powered the window halfway down and let her sniff the cool, late summer air.

Sometimes, especially at night, spotting the left turn to the cabin amidst all the foliage could be tricky. So Tony had put a marker at the entrance—a dilapidated carousel horse, pole stuck in the ground, which he'd found in a shed after buying the property.

Then down the lane we went, pulling up and in, behind Tony's truck.

I gathered Sushi and the basket, and—feeling a little like Dorothy in Oz—climbed the few wooden steps to the porch, where I knocked at the door.

When it opened, Tony gazed at me with unabashed fondness, then partially closed the door. "As fetching as you look, miss, and as tempted as I am to invite you in, I already have a girlfriend, and she's going to be here any minute."

"Very funny," I said with a little laugh.

Sushi had already jumped from my arms to trot between our legs, looking for the love of her life—Rocky, Tony's mutt with his trademark black circle around one eye, recalling the dog the Little Rascals ran with.

Tony stepped to one side. "You really do look lovely, Brandy."

My cheeks turned pinker than my blush. "Thank you."

A pleasant, woodsy aroma greeted me as I entered, the cabin roomier than it appeared from the outside. To the left was a cozy area with a fireplace (unlit) faced by an overstuffed brown couch and matching recliner; to the right, a four-chair, round oak table shared space with a china hutch. A short hallway led to a single bedroom, tiny bath, and kitchen, with a small porch on the back.

Cozy.

The rustic walls showcased Tony's collecting interests—an assortment of antiquated wooden snowshoes and various fishing items, old rods, wicker creels, and nets, all nailed there rather haphazardly.

Rocky knew the drill whenever Sushi arrived, and the bigger dog flopped on his side on the braided rug and patiently let her crawl all over him and lick his face. She had no shame.

Of course, neither had I.

Soon, I was in the kitchen washing and prepping the

vegetables while Tony tended to the grill on the back porch, toasting some garlic bread along with the steaks.

Then we were seated at the table, enjoying the meal with a bottle of Merlot, as the sun slowly disappeared outside, a nice breeze coming in the open window, ruffling the curtains.

Tony and I had our own cabin drill—no talk of Mother, or his work, or politics. But we did have plenty of common interests, including movies, music, and sports. And when the conversation ran out, neither of us minded the silence.

But I could sense on what was feeling like a perfect night that something was bothering him. And later—the dishes washed, with us seated on the couch, his arm around me, Sushi curled up with Rocky in front of a fireplace flickering with flames now that the night had cooled off—I thought we should get whatever it was that was troubling him out in the open.

So I said, "What's up, doc?"

"Shows, does it?"

"Yep."

"Here I thought I had a pretty good poker face."

I asked the dreaded question. "Is it us?"

"What? No. No."

Had another mob contract been taken out on him? Was there some other wife in his past he hadn't told me about?

"Work?" I asked.

"Well, there's always that, but . . . no."

That left only Mother.

He reclaimed his arm, twisted toward me. "There's an inquiry that Vivian will have to face."

"About what?"

"Some of her actions—or inactions—in Antiqua."

"For instance?"

He sighed. "Not calling the FBI immediately when evidence indicated that Mayor Hatcher had been kidnapped."

"But he *wasn't* kidnapped," I pointed out.

"This is procedure I'm talking about," Tony replied. "Whether or not the man really was kidnapped is moot. She also failed to instruct forensics to go over the mayor's car."

Mother had skipped that step, true enough. "What else?"

"She didn't have the authority to go outside regular law enforcement channels and involve the Sauk Nation, who were in another county."

I said defensively, "If she hadn't called them, Pastor Creed would have died."

"We don't know that. Now Serenity County is going to have to reimburse the tribe, which won't be cheap. And there's more."

This was starting to sound like a terrible infomercial.

He was saying, "I needn't remind you her driver's license was revoked long ago. So there's the little matter of her driving to the casino by herself, which showed up on the parking lot security cam."

I sighed. "I knew about that."

"Did you also know that she won over a hundred thousand dollars on that visit?"

"What? No!"

He was nodding. "Of course, she's donating it to the Sauk health clinic, but still . . . Vivian was gambling while acting at the time in a law enforcement capacity."

I sighed. "Anything else?"

"Well, there were no eyewitnesses, so it can't be proved, but . . ."

"But *what?*"

"Three farm mailboxes were casualties along the highway to the casino."

"That *does* sound like Mother," I admitted.

"And she owes the Antiqua city hall a new chalkboard. I realize she would have returned it, if that train hadn't hit your lodgings. Still."

"Please tell me you're finished."

"Not quite. There's a matter of a dozen complementary cartons of TAB soft drink being delivered to her at the Sheriff's Department from the Coca-Cola Company. When I heard about *that*, I told her that accepting any gifts could be seen as a bribe."

"And what did she say?"

"Put it on my tab."

I laughed despite myself.

But then suddenly it didn't seem so funny. "Were you the one who . . . ?"

Tony looked hurt. "Ratted her out? No, Brandy. This inquiry came about because of the report she filed, in which she detailed her own actions."

"Oh. Well, at least she's honest about it all."

"More like proud. She's almost certainly going to be called to come before the county commissioner, who will assess her actions and decide if any laws have been broken. If that results in a hearing, I could have to testify about what I know."

I sighed. "I understand."

He took my hand. Squeezed gently. "I just wanted you to know what's coming at you."

"I guess it's better than a train," I said. Then I brightened. "Hey, if she has to resign or whatever, I'm perfectly fine with that."

"You are?"

"Sure." I put my head on his shoulder. "And she loves doing jail time—between research and forming drama groups, that's like a vacation to her. Anyway, if she's not sheriff anymore, my life will be a whole lot better."

Or would it?

To be continued . . .

A Trash 'n' Treasures Tip

Shady book dealers will make a photo of a book too light in order to hide ageing or discoloration, or too dark to make defects invisible. Which Mother abhors where books are concerned, but she considers it a good practice for women of a certain age getting their pictures taken.

About the Authors

Barbara Allan is a joint pseudonym of husband-and-wife mystery writers Barbara and Max Allan Collins.

BARBARA COLLINS made her entrance into the mystery field as a highly respected short story writer with appearances in over a dozen top anthologies, including *Murder Most Delicious*, *Women on the Edge*, *Deadly Housewives*, and the best-selling *Cat Crimes* series. She was the co-editor of (and a contributor to) the best-selling anthology *Lethal Ladies*, and her stories were selected for inclusion in the first three volumes of *The Year's 25 Finest Crime and Mystery Stories*.

Two acclaimed hardcover collections of her work have been published: *Too Many Tomcats* and (with her husband) *Murder—His and Hers*. The Collins's first novel together, the Baby Boomer thriller *Regeneration*, was a paperback bestseller; their second collaborative novel, *Bombshell*—in which Marilyn Monroe saves the world from World War III—was published in hardcover to excellent reviews. Both are back in print under their "Barbara Allan" byline.

Barbara also has been the production manager and/or line producer on several independent film projects emanating from the production company she and her husband run.

MAX ALLAN COLLINS was named a Grand Master by the Mystery Writers of America in 2017. He has earned an unprecedented twenty-three Private Eye Writers of America "Shamus" nominations, many for his Nathan Heller historical thrillers, winning for *True Detective*

(1983), *Stolen Away* (1991), and the short story "So Long, Chief."

His classic graphic novel *Road to Perdition* is the basis of the Academy Award–winning film. Max's other comics credits include *Dick Tracy*; *Batman*; his own *Ms. Tree*; and *Wild Dog*, featured on the *Arrow* TV series.

Max's body of work includes film criticism, short fiction, songwriting, trading card sets, and movie/TV tie-in novels, such as the *New York Times* best sellers *Saving Private Ryan,* numerous *USA Today* best-selling CSI novels, and the Scribe Award–winning *American Gangster*. His nonfiction includes the current *Scarface and the Untouchable: Al Capone, Eliot Ness and the Battle for Chicago* (with A. Brad Schwartz).

An award-winning filmmaker, he wrote and directed the Lifetime movie *Mommy* (1996) and three other features; his produced screenplays include the 1995 HBO World Premiere *The Expert* and *The Last Lullaby* (2008). His 1998 documentary *Mike Hammer's Mickey Spillane* appears on the Criterion Collection release of the acclaimed film noir, *Kiss Me Deadly*. The Cinemax TV series *Quarry* is based on his innovative book series.

Max's recent novels include a dozen-plus works begun by his mentor, the late mystery-writing legend, Mickey Spillane, among them *Killing Town* with Mike Hammer and the Caleb York western novels.

"BARBARA ALLAN" live(s) in Muscatine, Iowa, their Serenity-esque hometown. Son Nathan works as a translator of Japanese to English, with credits ranging from video games to novels.